Dr. Hackenbush
Gets a Job

Ginger Mayerson

The Wapshott Press

Dr. Hackenbush Gets a Job

Published by
The Wapshott Press
PO Box 31513
Los Angeles, CA 90031

The Wapshott Press
www.WapshottPress.com

Copyright © 2002 and 2010 by Ginger Mayerson

First printing March 2010

ISBN: 978-0-9825813-0-8

06 05 04 03   4 3 2 1

Wapshott Press logo by Molly Kiely

Cover design by Robin Austin

Author's Preface

Long ago, in the mid 1980s, I was working a boring temp job at the old Red Cross building on Wilshire in Westlake. Nothing against boring temp jobs, they can be very restful, but this one was so boring, I began to mull over the story that would become *Dr. Hackenbush Gets a Job* and the other novels about Hackenbush and her milieu. I'd been playing the baritone ukulele to amuse myself and toying with the idea of starting a band. This never actually happened because writing chamber music was taking up all my spare time and energy. So I was living the Hackenbushian life of losing sleep due to working a day job and making music in every other possible moment, but not in nightclubs or at casual gigs. I had many of the same experiences of meeting people in offices who had been in the arts and were either relieved or regretful that they no longer were, or people who didn't really understand the life I was living, but were interested and sympathetic. They came to concerts and sometimes became friends. And so while I wasn't writing the Hackenbush saga, I was certainly thinking about it.

Around 2000, I ran out of things to say as a composer and stopped writing music, thought a few things over, and then segued into writing prose. Thank God for the internet because I was lucky to meet other writers online and learned the basics, wrote very bad things that got useful critiques and found the love and editorial support to write the Hackenbush novels and everything else. After writing the three Hackenbush novels I'd been mulling over for fifteen or so years, I began the long agent query quest. Dr. Hackenbush found a fan in William Reiss at John Hawkins Literary Agency, and bless him, Bill went above and beyond to find a publisher for *Dr. Hackenbush Gets a Job*. I've quoted a few of the editorial responses on the back cover. Having been in music, I thrive on rejection, but I must say that at this level, rejection is damn near self-esteem boosting.

But, if you're reading this, you know that *Dr. Hackenbush Gets a Job* has finally been published, and there are many people to thank for that. The endlessly patient Jane Seaton, who's read and edited my work from the very beginning while offering nothing but good advice and encouragement. Laurel Sutton, who's read, edited, and was the wind beneath my wings in the agent hunt. Lynn Loper, the strictest, most patient proofreader in the world. More recently, thank you to Robin Austin for the beautiful Hackenbush.org website and the cover of this book, and Kris Anderson, Molly Kiley, and Kathryn L. Ramage for three (count 'em, three) more proofreads before publication. And last but certainly not least, Bill Reiss, my wonderful agent, who liked this novel enough to inspire me not to give up on getting it published somewhere, someday, which is here and now. Thank you, everyone, this book would not have seen the light of day without you all.

And if I did dedications, I would dedicate this book to anyone who's ever had to work a day job when they'd rather be making art.

Ginger Mayerson
January 2010

Dr. Hackenbush
Gets a Job

Yeah, it was a bad night. Ended up that way. Started out a good night. No intonation problems, nobody late or too stoned to play right, Shorty was dancing like an angel, and even Wang the Bartender was in a good mood.

And then Hackenbush watched it all go to hell, even assisted it into hell. But what's a lady to do when some gorilla in a plaid shirt attacks your dance partner?

"Say, fella, you wouldn't hit a girl wearing glasses, would you?" Edging between a mountain of drunk and Shorty, Hackenbush pointed at her big, black horn rims. This brought out the buried chivalry in the drunk; he snatched her baritone ukulele and crunched it up instead of her nose.

It's always such a shame when one must sacrifice one's baritone ukulele to an enraged bar patron, but there are times when it's just fucking necessary. Either that or watch Shorty get his jaws busted.

The ensuing brawl was quick and to the point: the drunk, joined by other drunks, tore the Lotus Room bar of the New Hotel Watanabe to bits. Luckily, no lives, instruments, except the baritone, or musicians were lost.

"So, Wang," Hackenbush began after the police were gone, "see ya tomorrow?" She lit an unfiltered Pall Mall and picked a shred of tobacco off her tongue.

"I think not, Hackenbush."

Hackenbush followed Wang's gaze over her left shoulder and was face to face with her favorite club owner, the fabulous Mr. Hikaru Tanaka.

"Oh, Mr. Tanaka!" Hackenbush enthused with more energy than she felt. "How nice to see you."

Tanaka looked around at the wreckage, the musicians packing up, Shorty Smith and Hackenbush and raised his voice: "This bar is closed until further notice."

It was bad enough, but then Hackenbush had to take a

cab home because her ancient convertible Karmann-Ghia would start and keep running, but not move forward in any gear.

Tow trucks were not Hackenbush's enemy. The reason for calling a tow truck—that was the enemy. Or maybe just nemesis. Or bad luck. Or simply that the good luck that kept the wrecks Hackenbush drove running just finally did what good luck eventually does, which is pack up, and then you call a tow truck. So, Hackenbush called a tow truck the next morning to tow her car to her mechanic.

She thanked God for Auto Club even though, after the last tow, they had suggested her car problems were more than their organization could help her with. So even Auto Club comes to the end of its good will eventually. Auto Club and Mr. Tanaka had just about had enough Hackenbush.

'He'll get over it,' she thought, climbing out of the tow truck. She waved at Roberto, VW mechanic and sole proprietor. "Hopefully."

"What?" The tow driver was a stocky, swarthy bear of a man and thought he'd misheard.

"I said hopefully he'll get over it." Hackenbush handed him her AAA card.

"Who?"

"Vice President Bush." Hackenbush signed her trip sheet or whatever the hell it was one signed after a tow. "He seems so angry. Rich angry white guy who wants to be President of the US. Hopefully he'll get over it. How'd you vote in the last election?" She wrestled a cigarette out of the pack and lit it.

"Communist." He handed her back her Auto Club card.

"Really? What a shocking waste of time." She picked a shred of tobacco off her tongue.

"Not in Yerevan." The driver waved gallantly, speeding off to rescue the next paid-up Auto Club damsel in distress. A dead bug; old VWs were most of his business, so he liked them.

"Making friends, Hackenbush?" Roberto looked up from the back of her Ghia.

"I try to be a ray of sunshine in the life of everyone I meet," she said, and then decided to stub out her cigarette in street, far away from the gas hoses Roberto was waving around.

"I think I have bad news for you, sunshine," Roberto said, when she got back. "Looks like the tranny died."

"Couldn't it just be tranny fluid?" He showed her the suitably pink dipstick. "Ah. What's a Ghia tranny cost these days?"

"A thousand and takes a couple of days."

"It's gonna take me more than a couple of days to get a thousand bucks together." And pay the rent, and buy a new uke, and find a new steady money gig, and...

"How long?"

"If I can get a temp gig right away, couple of weeks; maybe more," she said, after a review of her finances, which didn't take long, and who she could tap for a loan, which took even less time. "What'll you charge me for storage?"

"If you can get it outta here in three weeks, it's on the house."

"Ah, Christmas is early this year." She gave his arm a grateful squeeze. "Four weeks?"

"Check back in three. See how I'm feeling." Roberto closed the trunk.

"Give me a lift down to Wilshire?" Hackenbush tapped up a smoke and offered it to him.

"Sorry, my driver's picking up parts in the valley." He accepted the cigarette. "Bus that goes downtown stops across the street there. You can get a westbound at Wilshire and Fig."

Get it, yes; like it, no. "Can you give me change for a five?" she asked politely.

"Well, that I can do."

It was a shame that Hackenbush was unable to look down in a moving vehicle without getting nauseated. It meant she couldn't read on the bus and had time to think.

Thinking while driving has a necessarily superficial quality to it. One is driving, after all, and crashing due to thinking too hard doesn't go over well with the insurance company. Hackenbush never crashed her cars; they crashed internally or other cars crashed into them while parked. And it was hard to think in the go-carts she drove while part of her was willing it into continuing motion, moment by moment, mile by mile.

So she dreaded the bus. Not the company, nor the wasted time, nor the plastic seats, nor the scratched windows; none of that really bothered her. It was the hours she'd spend catching up on all the thinking she wasn't doing in the car or anywhere else.

How was Hackenbush, at age thirty-one, unable to pull together two thousand dollars on short notice? Or even fifteen hundred? Was her luck running out again? Why was she living on luck anyway? Savings: what a concept.

And the review went on and on. It helped to focus on the concrete. On the plus side, she had two hundred in the savings, a hundred in checking, about eighty in cash, a check coming for the past week at the Lotus Room (Tanaka was pissed, but he wouldn't hold up the band's money) out of which she would get five hundred.

On the down side she needed a grand for the car, two hundred for a new baritone ukulele, and then more money for rent, food, and transportation. And to get all this, she needed gigs, and lots of them, to keep her going. She couldn't gig until she got a new uke. Well, she could, but she got fewer just-singing jobs. Clubs and caterers hired *Dr. Hackenbush and her Orchestra* and that included a baritone ukulele, which she didn't have just then.

That left temp jobs. They were okay as long as they paid well and didn't go on too long. They were okay if there were any around. One thing in her favor was that it was only February and the students would all be in school or working nights and weekends only. That left a fairly good field of office jobs. Typing jobs. Jobs where you're worshipped if you can just get there on time. And if you can function, well, you might be elevated from idol to deity by lunchtime.

Temp jobs: friend or foe? She'd worked jobs at big, monster companies where temps had been there as long as eight years. They might yet still be there. After eight years, they ought to hire that person, retroactive by seven years. But it just didn't work that way. A temp stayed on her toes or she (or he) was out. Eight years is a long time to be on your toes with no benefits. Or maybe they had benefits; Hackenbush had heard of agencies that would let you buy some benefits after a while. Yeah, buy; they're making sixty percent on top of your hourly labor and you can buy something they ought to give you if they had a decent...

"Oh thank God," Hackenbush groaned as the bus jerked to a stop and she could stop thinking this bullshit.

"For what?" the driver asked.

"It's not raining." They watched a shower start. "Ah. It's so good for the crops."

"Right, lady. Have a good day."

"Yeah, thanks buddy, you too." She hopped off the bus and dashed for the minimal awning across the sidewalk. Architects in Los Angeles either didn't believe in wet weather or never rode the bus or both. Anyway, no point in waiting for it slack off; LA rain never did when you needed it to—it could always outwait you. Lucky that Temporary Insanity was close by; sometimes fate let you outsmart the rain. Ha ha.

Anna Kodaly ran Temporary Insanity out of a couple of hundred square feet in one of the more modest and elderly towers on Wilshire between Westlake and Korea Town. It was cheap and cheerful; the building being neither new nor sleek suited Anna and her clientele down to the ground. She dealt in other peoples' needs; understaffed offices and cash-strapped free-lance secretaries preferred to face their problems without the distraction of pretentious décor and a fashionable address. Unlike her clients, Kodaly didn't need much in the way of an office, just phone and file space mainly. She was glad to have it after trying to work out of her apartment where a bad case of cabin fever took care of that idea for good.

So, the sole proprietor of Temporary Insanity looked up at the damp and bedraggled Hackenbush pushing open the door and smiled. It was always nice to see Hackenbush. Nice for Anna, meant she'd make a few bucks off the Hackenbush secretarial magic; not so nice for Hackenbush, who was usually in a jam.

Kodaly had worked for a big agency before opening her own. In that time she'd noticed a few things, such as the best temps were usually in the arts and not making much money there. They were the ones who could find the address, get there, do the job and even leave a good, often excellent, impression. But to leave was the important thing; these people did good work because it was a short-term thing and didn't completely demoralize them.

So Anna saved her money and opened Temporary Insanity, casually letting a few of her best temps know where they could find her. They did and they sent their friends. Anna was unusual in that she could handle a cash-strapped and frustrated artist with grace and charm, and the artists loved her for it. She built a steady little business on placing actresses on phones, which they answered with well modulated, dulcet tones; poets on word processors, where they typed like furies and composed grammatical letters; and dancers rising on their powerful legs to usher well-heeled clients into boardrooms and even glide cheerfully away to get coffee for eleven (hey, it beat the hell out of being a waitress). And all the while these efficient, overeducated, often brilliant people were dreaming of their own work and bringing the focus, brains and perfectionism of that creative work into offices all over Los Angeles. Such workers were impressive, appreciated and gone, gone, gone as soon as they'd saved enough to get the hell out there. Thanks for the dough and the free coffee, see ya. Too smart for their day jobs, but not smart enough or lucky enough or whatever enough to make a living at their real work.

But even among the best of the best on Kodaly's books, Hackenbush stood out. Her bosses not only liked her and her work, they respected her. Hell, most of them went to hear her sing at least once. Hackenbush was impressive; she got things done, she anticipated what was needed, worked well under pressure, could follow even the stupidest instructions, worked hard and long hours when needed and was reliable. She gave everyone she knew the feeling that it was all under control And she was exactly what Kodaly needed at Withers and

Sons, and needed now.

So her smile was part pleasure, part relief and a splash of regret when Hackenbush settled into the interviewee chair before her desk. "Heard about the Lotus Room, Mabel; sorry."

"Man, the word gets around, don't it, Anna?" Hackenbush accepted the proffered cigarette and ripped the filter off. "That scene happened less than twelve hours ago." A study in studied cool, she was tidying up the ripped end before she put it in her mouth.

"Your bass player's wife called first thing and needs a job until he finds another gig," Kodaly told her. "I hear it was Shorty's fault."

"Only that a mean drunk went after him." Hackenbush blew out a lungful of smoke and pinched a piece of tobacco off her tongue.

"And you got in the middle of it."

"I thought I could talk him out of it," Hackenbush said, tired of the subject. "I didn't know smashing up my uke was just a prelude to smashing up the bar."

"You could have stayed out of it."

"Yeah, well, and he hurts Shorty, who, like me, has no health insurance, and then smashes up the bar and I'm still out of work and a gutless coward to boot." Hackenbush stubbed out her mutilated cigarette and lit one of her own. "Better this way. I can't pay for the car with my guts, but I do sleep better at night."

"What's with your wheels?" Kodaly asked, mentally reviewing the bus lines between chez Hackenbush and Withers and Sons.

"The transmission died last night." Hackenbush winced a little; Kodaly was a good lady, but you never want to be too much at anybody's mercy.

"All at once?"

"They're like men, Anna; sometimes they warn you before they go, sometimes they just go."

"I must remember that." Kodaly was grimly amused and recalled that Hackenbush had not been so blasé when Eddy Lee dumped her four years ago. Ah well. "When it rains it pours," she said, reaching the file she'd had on her desk for the past three weeks.

"Comes in threes," Hackenbush said.

"Oh? The bar is closed, your car is dead; what's the third?"

"My baritone ukulele got smashed."

"Oh, yes, you did say that." Kodaly looked up. "I could lend you a hundred or so for a new one."

"Thanks, maybe later. Still got that job you called me about three weeks ago?"

"As a matter of fact, I do. Can you start this afternoon?"

"Ah. Progress," thought Hackenbush. She was momentarily relieved, but then got suspicious. "Your client waited three weeks for me?" she asked.

"Not exactly. You'll be taking over from somebody who wants to leave."

"Why do they want to leave? Eleven bucks an hour is good money for a secretary job these days." She watched Anna close the file folder and sigh. Hackenbush sighed too, just to keep her company.

"Here the scoop, Mabel: I've had seven temps in there in the past three weeks," Kodaly said, looking right into Hackenbush's deceptively bland eyes. It was her 'listening to the deal' look; it meant she'd take the job, but needed all the facts. "These guys are a little goofy at this place. Not really mean, but playful."

"What kind of playful?" Hackenbush asked, figuring if she could handle drunks (sort of), club owners, guitar players...

'Well, they're not ass grabbers," Kodaly said. "They're booby trappers."

"That's worse, Anna, now c'mon..."

"No, no, I mean they set traps around the office," Kodaly quickly explained.

"They what?"

"Set traps, you know, snares. Like changing the character set to Chinese on the computer, putting envelopes so they fall when the cabinet is opened, taking the add key off the calculator, telling a dirty joke on the Dictaphone. Things like that."

"Huh. Weird." Hackenbush sat smoking, mulling it over.

"Paula Dreisler is the office manager there," Kodaly said at last. "She asked for you."

"Oh, is that where she landed," Hackenbush drawled just a little too coolly. "She hates me for replacing her as the best singer in town." Then she choked on the smoke she was exhaling.

"Good thing she didn't call you for your modesty, Hackenbush."

"She quit."

"She quit the clubs for a steady money job."

"She chickened out."

"Unlike you, she had a kid to support. She didn't ask to be a widow."

"Ah, thanks, Anna. I like feeling like a heel."

"Only when you are one." Kodaly stubbed out her cigarette and leaned over her desk. "Look, Mabel, take this job. It will accomplish many things for many people. You'll make me a hero, you'll rescue the poor devil that's there now, you'll help Paula out and fuck knows you need the money. So check your ego for a while and go make eleven bucks an hour." She leaned back and opened the file again. "And just think, dearie, the sooner you make enough to get your car fixed, the sooner you can return to being the best singer in town. Before somebody usurps your crown."

"Fuck you, Anna." Hackenbush laughed for the first time that day. "Where is this place?"

"Catty corner from Otis on Wilshire."

"Well, at least I can drink at La Fonda on my lunch hour if necessary." She jotted the address in her notebook. "It's a law firm? I'm not a legal secretary."

"You're not getting paid to be one," Anna said, shoving time cards at her. "They just need somebody smart, reliable and with nerves of steel. You choose to live in Lincoln Heights, you drive an old, old VW and you fight drunks twice your size; that qualifies you on the nerves of steel part."

"I live in Lincoln Heights because it's what I can afford,

same reason I drive old VWs," Hackenbush said. "I only fight giant drunks under extreme duress."

Anna waved it off; she'd heard it before. "Speaking of money, do you need some cash for lunch and bus fare?"

"No thanks, I've got my share of last night's tip jar."

"An advance?"

"Not now, I've got a check coming from the club." Hackenbush looked out at the rain. "Now that I'm a pedestrian, I could use an umbrella."

Kodaly handed her a stubby black one and wished her luck.

"Well, I can always use that." Hackenbush waved at her and headed for the eastbound bus. She could start this job just in time for lunch.

On superficial acquaintance it was hard to know whether Hackenbush wore big, black horn-rim glasses to hide the fact there was a pretty lady under there, or to obscure the fact that there wasn't.

Dreisler was pondering this after Kodaly called to give her the good news. Well, it was good news. Withers Junior's secretary had quit in a fit of pique and they were short-handed. This meant the office was in chaos. It wasn't so much Hackenbush's office skills Dreisler needed, it was the lady's commanding, no-bullshit bandleader presence to keep the office in line until a new secretary could be hired. The last applicant had fled when Withers Senior chased the temp before this one through the office in his wheelchair. That Dreisler's nineteen-year-old son, Bobby, had been pushing Withers Senior's chariot jumped up the office manager's anxiety, too. This was a good job; she'd even deal with a poseur siren like Hackenbush to keep it.

It was good news, of sorts, when Bobby came home far too late the previous night and told his mother that the Lotus Room was trashed and Hackenbush out of work. Little Bobby's crush on Hackenbush was worrying for Dreisler, but economic necessity won out and she resigned herself to throwing them together (where she could keep an eye on them). Additionally, it might be sobering for Bobby to see his goddess under fluorescent lights eight hours a day, and thus Hackenbush's sojourn at Withers and Sons might be doubly beneficial. So, in the swirl of chaos Withers and Sons had become, she was pondering the glasses question for the nth time when the object of her meditation walked in like she owned the joint. "Ah," Paula thought, rising from the reception desk to greet her, "how positively Hackenbush."

"So glad you could make it, Hackenbush."

"So glad it was here to make, Dreisler," Hackenbush drawled. "I thought you were the office manager, not the receptionist."

"I cover where I'm needed, Mabel," Paula said, leading her down the hallway.

Linda Lim practically fell at Hackenbush's feet when the singers strolled up to her desk. Linda was a sculptor and more acclimated to the silence of her studio. The Withers and Sons madhouse had nearly done in her delicate sensibilities over the past week. "Oh, thank God, Mabel," she said, "I nearly died of joy when Anna called and–" She cut herself off seeing Dreisler's stern face.

"Now, now, Linda," Dreisler murmured. "We don't want to frighten Hackenbush, do we?"

"No, of course not," Linda said firmly and equally firmly added that she'd do anything, anything at all, to get out of there so Hackenbush could take over.

Dreisler said nothing and, even though it was only Thursday, paid her for the whole week. It certainly wasn't Linda's fault she couldn't manage these incorrigible guys. Now, if she could have used her stone hammer on them...hm, well, it just didn't bear thinking about.

"Helluvan artist," Hackenbush said, watching Linda bolt for the elevator. "Her last show simply knocked me sideways."

"I saw the catalogue," Dreisler said. "Very impressive."

"So, why am I here, Paula?"

"Temporary Insanity didn't have any out of work lion tamers," Dreisler admitted. "You're as close as I could get."

"How bad is it?"

"Oh, not that bad. This firm makes a pile off its

corporate clients so there's either a lot of work or it's really slow. And when it's slow, like now, the lawyers get bored and, ah, feisty." Dreisler pulled up the client base and codes on the computer. "These guys are a little strange, but generous if you do good work."

"Strange, like, how?"

Hearing her son returning with sandwiches for the office lunch, Dreisler angled her body so he wouldn't see Hackenbush when he went by. That would have to wait; Dreisler wanted to get Hackenbush up to speed as quickly as she could. "Well, Charles Withers Senior has been in a wheelchair since before I came here," she said. "He no longer goes to court, but he's still sharp as a tack."

"And a shark?"

"Pretty much all of them are sharks."

"How many is all and how many do I work for?"

"Three. Withers Senior, Withers Junior and Withers Other, also known as Frank," Dreisler said. "You work for Withers Junior, but help us all out when you've got downtime. It's either feast or famine with Withers Junior You'll either be dying of boredom or dying of overwork. We pay overtime and if you can calm this joint down, I'll try to get you a bonus."

"You're my hero, Paula," Hackenbush said, offering Dreisler a cigarette, lighting it and lighting one for herself. "What the fuck is a 'Withers Other'?" she asked, picking a piece of tobacco off her tongue.

"Younger, half-brother, to Junior," Dreisler paused to inhale deeply, relishing a decent, straightforward smoke for a change. "A nice guy, does more of the boring law; liaison with the patent lawyers, trademarks, wills, labor board actions, employee lawsuits against our clients—that kind of stuff."

"All law is boring to me so I'll take your word for it," Hackenbush said, rooting around the desk for an ashtray. She came up with nothing but a coffee cup so they flicked their ashes into that.

"Thanks." Dreisler tapped the ash off her smoke and noticed a few more gray hairs in Hackenbush's dark brown mop that hadn't been there last time she'd seen her. "But I'm sure I have more and time goes by for all of us, even Hackenbush," she thought, mechanically explaining the hours and office guidelines to Hackenbush.

"Doctor Hackenbush."

Tones of awe. Bobby's voice. It was an act of pure will for Dreisler not to throw herself protectively between her cub and the diva. Or at least not claw at Hackenbush's face.

"Hiya, kid, howareya?" Hackenbush recognized him, but damn if she could haul up his name. "What are you doing here? Did the restaurant close, too?"

"Restaurant?" Dreisler asked.

"Yeah, kid buses tables at the Storm Hill restaurant and hangs near the bar on his breaks," Hackenbush said, picking out one of the remaining sandwiches proffered and declining Bobby's offer to run out and get her anything, ANYTHING, she wanted.

"Oh, really?"

"Yes, ma'am, that's as close as I can get to *Dr. Hackenbush and her Orchestra*." Bobby winked at Hackenbush, who winked back. "I work here days."

"Oh, how nice," Hackenbush said. "Paula Dreisler's a helluva singer. You should dig up some of her old records sometime."

"Oh, I know. She's my mom."

"NO!"

"Yes!"

"NO!"

"Yes. Bobby, you have things to do," Dreisler cut off whatever her son was going to say.

"See you, Bobby," Hackenbush said, filing the name away for future use. "Let's do lunch," she added with a wink. "So that's your son, Paula," she said when he was gone. "He's cute."

"No, he's not," Dreisler snarled.

"Okay, he's not cute." Hackenbush examined her sandwich. "Does lunch usually come with this gig?"

"Not always. Withers Junior finished the prelims on a merger today and was feeling big and generous." Dreisler handed her a stack of tiny Dictaphone tapes. "You can start with these. I'll introduce you around the office when everyone's digesting their lunch and suitably mellow." She exited on Hackenbush's polite laugh and went to the mailroom, also known as Bobbyville.

Dreisler approached her son, who was approaching his ham on rye. "Bobby, how long have you been bussing tables at the Storm Hill?"

"Almost a year. Wang the bartender helped me get the job."

"I see." Dreisler leaned on the copy machine. "Why?"

"He got tired of tossing me out of the bar," Bobby said around bites. "He was worried about the liquor license."

"And all this just to be near Hackenbush." Dreisler shook her head sadly.

"Be near her singing, ma. Y'ever heard her sing?"

"Once or twice."

"She lights up the room."

"Does she?"

"And I've been stealing her phrasing. You like the way I play *Stardust* these days; that's the Hackenbush influence," he said over his shoulder as he went out to collect files.

There was truth in this, Dreisler had to admit. Over the past year Bobby had gone from a competent guitarist to an inspired one. That this was due to Hackenbush made her wince, but oh well, the Hackenbush ought to be good for something other than annoyance factor.

Transcription from Dictaphone was one of the few typing tasks Hackenbush almost enjoyed. One had to stay focused on the work and the hours simply melted away. And when one gets paid by the hour, one wants them to melt away.

However, there's no accounting for interruptions. Especially when they hover, expectantly, in the peripheral vision. Only waiters have mastered selective tunnel vision. Poor Hackenbush was merely a musician, used to noticing cues from other musicians and the odd conductor here and there, and had no control over her peripheral vision. She was doomed to look up, and look up she did.

Well, at least he wasn't hard on the eyes. Medium height, triangle build; creamy, coppery skin you could practically ski on. In a turban and embroidered vest he'd do for an Arabian nights fantasy (as if she could be bothered with fantasy any more). Or without them. He was cute with a kind of distinguished edginess that Hackenbush associated with a tenuous grip on your socio-economic status and a deep and abiding need to keep up appearances. Ah, here was someone who cared enough about what other people thought that he might even be able to see their point of view and weigh their opinion, but only as it pertained to himself.

Resigned to action, Hackenbush took her foot off the Dictaphone pedal and a headphone off one ear and generated an interested look on her face. He said, "Hi," in a soft tenor that she thought was kind of cute. It had just enough whine in it to sound like a request for tolerance, if not approval.

But this was not the basso voice on the tape, Withers Junior's voice, or so she was told, so Hackenbush had no idea who this person was. She said, "Hi," just to be polite and waited for things to develop.

"I'm Frank Withers," he said eventually.

"Ah, one of the Brothers Withers?" Mabel worked up enough interest to ask.

"Half brother," he said.

"Half full or half empty?"

"Excuse me?"

"Sorry, never mind; it made sense before I said it." Hackenbush knew she was tired of a conversation when wit, his or hers, both or either, failed her. She adjusted the headband of her headphones meaningfully, wishing he'd go away and let her get on with transcribing the utterly fascinating real estate deal on the tape.

Smart guy or maybe sensitive, possibly polite or just able to see when a lady doesn't want to talk, Frank seemed to get the message, but didn't move. "I just wanted to introduce myself."

"Thank you."

"Bobby said your name is Mabel, but everyone calls you Dr. Hackenbush."

"That's true, Mr. Withers," she said, wondering how she could scare him away before he could ask...

"What kind of doctor are you?"

She leaned forward and looked around suspiciously. "Bobby didn't tell you?" she asked in hushed tones.

"No," he hissed in enthusiastic hushed tones.

"Go ask him." She leaned back and smiled.

"I did, he said he didn't know."

"Huh, well he might not," Hackenbush admitted, tired of the game. "Here's the story: when I was a little girl I saw "Day at the Races", and in that one, Groucho is a vet named Dr. Hackenbush. I thought that was so great, I, all of five years old, announced to my father that I, too, would be a vet named Dr. Hackenbush."

"And did you become a vet?"

"Nah, but the nickname stuck and it's a good hook for the band. Dr. Hackenbush and her Orchestra is memorable for some reason," she said.

"Well, I'll never forget it." Frank smiled. It was a nice smile, interested without being overly nosy and somewhat on the timid side.

Hackenbush smiled back, suspecting this guy probably didn't meet many musicians and why should he? Most lounge lizards didn't have to work in offices. "So, anyway, Mr. Withers—"

"Please call me Frank. Mr. Withers is so formal."

"And it takes so long to say, Frank," she smiled at him. "And your brother? Should I call him Chuck or Charlie?"

"Well, he's a little more formal than I am," Frank said slowly. "You might want to start out with Mr. Withers and see where it goes."

"Then I will. Is he coming to introduce himself, too?"

"He's with clients all afternoon," Frank said, waving a zaftig blonde over. "Won't be back until tomorrow. Adela," he said to the blonde. "This is Dr. Hackenbush."

"Pleased to meet you, Doctor," she said, handing a stack of papers to Frank.

"Oh, just call me Hackenbush or Mabel. I answer to either."

"Lemme know if you need anything, Mabel," Adela said. "Unfortunately, right now I need my boss to get on with his chores."

"He's all yours, Adela." Hackenbush silently blessed her blonde-but-dark-at-the-roots savior leading the errant attorney back to his office as she sat back down to her typing. Ah, typing; just you and the machine and whatever bullshit was in the headphones.

Five o'clock seemed to come right away, so Hackenbush ignored it and worked until six thirty. There was plenty to do and the bus ride home might not be any shorter, but odds were it would be less crowded. She had to stand for most of it, which was fine because she was too tired to think heavy-duty thoughts and too busy watching her back. A French percussionist once told her French guidebooks for the Untied States advise visitors not to make eye contact in the cities. Well, Hackenbush made eye contact, tired eye contact with the tired eyes around her. These bus riders were just too damn weary after eight-plus-hour shifts to start anything. Rage and aggression were for those with the energy for it. And they were not on the eastbound Wilshire bus that rainy evening.

At Third and Broadway, she caught the northbound bus through Chinatown and into Lincoln Heights. She got off at North Broadway and Johnston, bought two packs of cigarettes at Big Saver and walked past the Post Office toward home. She lit a smoke out of habit, out of need from the long ride in the bus and out of the fantasy that if she were attacked, she might buy herself some time singeing her assailant. A kind of tobacco-Aikido. Mostly she smoked as she walked those last few blocks home to keep herself company. Nobody menaced her; in fact, she met no one on that evening. It was too early or too late, or all the action was over on Eastlake street that evening. Didn't matter; Hackenbush finally relaxed when she got home and shot the deadbolt behind her.

There are lots of kinds of tired, but this was not them; this was drained, wrung out, dead-on-her-feet weary. It was what the first day of sitting on her ass typing did every time. Hackenbush knew she'd get over it, build up a tolerance to it, but, man, the first day of a temp job was pure hell. Well, actually, the aftermath and letdown were hell; the job itself was just boring. Thrashed though she was, she cleared her answering machine out of habit. Anna Kodaly called to see how it went; Hackenbush would call her tomorrow, from work. Shorty called to see if she was still alive; she'd call him tomorrow from work, too. Bruno Carlos called about a gig at the Island Room weekend after next; him she called back.

"I don't have a uke," she told him.

"I hear," he said, *Meditations* blaring in the background. "I hear you don' hava gig either, 's why I can get you for a weekend gig, diva baby."

"Excuse me, Carlos, but can you turn the fucking Coltrane off while you talk to me?" she yelled into the phone. "I mean, if you were listening to *Coltrane Sound* or those recordings with Monk, okay, but this stuff just–" she cut herself off in the sudden silence. "Hello?" She listened intently. "Fuck! I hope he didn't hang up." She was relieved to hear a match strike and a wheezy inhalation. "Good thing you play the congas, Bruno, you couldn't play an oxygen mask on those lungs," she thought as she lit up herself, but assumed Bruno had something more interesting to smoke. Might have been nice, but she didn't have any interesting stuff around and tomorrow was a work day after all.

"Jus' bring your beautiful self and more beautiful voice down to the Island Room on week from Sa'day at nine," Bruno drawled.

"Saturday or Sunday?"

"Sa'day at nine, my goddess."

"The twentieth or the twenty-first?" she said, digging her calendar out of her purse.

"Week from Sa'day."

"Fuck." She'd call the Island Room tomorrow and find out. "What's it pay?"

"Fifty, plus tips."

'The usual,' she thought. "Who else is in the band?"

"Only people you like, Hackenbush," he wheezed. "Bring Shorty, he amuses me."

"Can you pay him to amuse you?"

"He can take a cut of 's tip jar, no?"

"I'll ask."

"See you on Sa'day, my diva."

"Yeah yeah yeah." Hackenbush rolled her eyes at the dial tone and hung up. "A gig's a gig's a gig." It was merely the shank of the evening but, after making a quick to-do list for the next day and setting the alarm for the hellish hour of five forty-five am, she hit the sheets and slept the heavy, dream-free sleep exhausted secretaries sleep.

There is a particular kind of raw chill in the winter air at five forty-five am in Los Angeles. Cold with a touch of some acetone-like vapor that leaves the skin stripped and slightly burning. At least Hackenbush thought so, as she fought off the alarm clock and the almost overwhelming urge to roll back under the covers. But she was strong, she was invincible, and she had to get to work. And get there on the bus, which could take a while. She turned on the space heater by her bed on her way into the bathroom.

It was more trouble than it was worth to light the ancient gas heater in there. It usually gave her a headache before it warmed her up and the Gas Company warning sticker that they were not, absolutely not, completely not responsible if the "occupant(s)" asphyxiated their own stupid asses because they had been warned was also discouraging. Well, it was true, Hackenbush had been warned, so she let the water take the chill off and the gas heater stayed cold. The Department of Water and Power might despair of others, but they could be proud of how much Hackenbush took their drought warnings to heart. The singer put a bucket under the faucet to catch the water until it was warm enough to get under the shower, she'd use to water for plants or cleaning later, thereby conserving at least some gallons of city water over the course of the year. Possibly it went deeper than DWP's pamphlets; possibly, simply deep down Hackenbush knew that when there isn't enough, one conserves so there is some for everyone. Wasn't that being a good neighbor? Do unto others as you would... She showered quickly and rushed back into the electrically warmed bedroom to finish toweling her hair, which was well below her shoulders and needed to be cut, which would have to wait a while.

What a number of things would have to wait awhile until the rent and utilities were paid, the car fixed, a new ukulele purchased. She added a note to call around for prices on a baritone uke and see if she could get a brunette discount. Sometimes that worked, but usually in person. So she'd need a haircut to negotiate. "Oh well," she thought, filtering a cup of coffee and moving her insufficient funds around her expanding expenses like valet parking attendants moving Ferraris on a Friday night. She liked that metaphor even though she'd do almost anything not to pay for valet parking because that was something else she couldn't afford. In a city of cars, paying for parking was a little like being charged for oxygen. It pissed her off so much, she only did it under extreme duress and in certain parts of town, the more dangerous parts.

Hackenbush took a sip of coffee and lit her first cigarette of the day. She liked to wait until she could take that first blissful drag with a cup of coffee because it was especially divine that way. The rest of the day's smoking would never quite recapture the pleasure of the first half of the first cigarette, but the memory and nicotine withdrawal kept her trying and trying and never succeeding. But sometimes chemical necessity takes precedence over pure hedonism and Mabel Hackenbush was a realist down to her two-inch heel office pumps. Actually, she put the office shoes in a totebag, along with a book to read at lunch and her to-do list and some sheet music she was arranging for her combo, and marched off to the bus in a pair of cheap tennis shoes. She could face anything if her feet didn't hurt and was enough of an RTD rider to know that LA buses were dismal just-fucking-get-me-there vehicles and nobody cared about your shoes. She also wore a long, ratty overcoat to keep the grime off her second hand navy blue serge dress that the more pretentious observer would call 'vintage'. It was used clothing; good fabric, good styles and right in her price range. She could never afford this stuff new, so she went for vintage hip, not pricey status. Vintage hip was more affordable and you could haggle better in a downtown rag house than at Chanel.

It wasn't raining, but she kept Anna's umbrella handy as she bopped over to Griffin and Ave 28, where it did start to rain. She took the RTD into Chinatown where she hopped a DASH bus, for variety, down to Wilshire and then another RTD west to MacArthur Park. It was two fares instead of one and a bus transfer, but seemed a little faster to her. She'd try different routes, just to break up the monotony and so as not to have too much time to think about why she was riding the fucking bus at all. Even if she could afford to rent a car, she'd have to go to Enterprise, who, bless them, took cash deposits in lieu of credit cards, because she didn't have enough steady income for a credit card. So, okay, she had no debt; well, that was good. And if she had a credit card, it could be for emergencies like getting the car fixed or a new uke or all those records she'd been eyeing at Rockaway and a couple of new evening gowns from Saks Fifth Avenue, where you have to pay retail, for casual and country club gigs and... Okay, it was better that she didn't have a credit card; her life would become a continuous emergency if she did. But didn't Saks have a revolving charge account? "Aw, shit!"

"S'matter, miss?" the bus driver asked.

"I spaced my stop," she said, scanning in the rain for the next one.

"Don't tell anybody I did this," he said, opening the front door at a red light. "And don't get hit."

"You're a prince, daddy-o," she said, checking traffic and bolting for the curb. She decided the bus driver's compassion was a good omen, indicating that her luck was changing and it was blue skies and smooth sailing from here on out. It was pouring rain and her shoes were soaked by the time she got to the office. But her luck was changing; fuck her shoes.

She dashed into the building and was even able to get into an elevator just as the doors were closing. And found herself in a small space with a tall, slim, gorgeous male type of man with lovely blue eyes and just enough gray in his dark hair to set him squarely on the dishy side (to Hackenbush, who occasionally admired the distinguished, suit-wearing

types, of course only for aesthetic reasons because, well...
looking at men was really the only safe thing to do with
them). For his part, he was leisurely looking her over, too.
Hackenbush took a deep breath. These situations caused all
the stored-up nicotine to rush to her feet so she pulled a
mostly dry pack of cigarettes out of her pocket. "Say, buddy,
got a light?" she asked.

"No smoking in elevators," he said, taking the smoke
out of her fingers.

"And what are you, dad? The fire patrol?"

"Hardly," he said, putting the cigarette in his pocket.
"However, I am an officer of the court, if you need an
identifying characteristic."

"I'd say there's other identifying characteristics about
you I'd rather remember," Hackenbush told him as the
elevator shuddered to a stop.

"Good-bye, miss," he said with a smile and a nod.

She watched him walk away and just as the doors were
closing, realized he'd gotten off on Withers and Sons' floor.
She pressed a random button, the roof as it turned out, to give
her time to think. "An officer of the court," she mused as the
elevator ascended. It was early yet, so she stepped onto the
roof landing and lit a cigarette to keep her company.

Hackenbush liked being up in tall buildings. The one
she was on now was only six stories but, now that the rain had
stopped, gave her a clear view of downtown to the east,
Wilshire corridor to the west and parks—Macarthur and
Lafayette—on both sides. She liked this height: it felt like
she was in the city, not looming over it. It was a big flat roof;
bigger than most rehearsal halls and certainly cheaper—like,
free.

All this flitted through her mind just behind the largish
fact that she'd probably just been sassing her boss in the
elevator. She stubbed out her smoke and considered having
another, but decided she'd rather get her exit interview over
with. Fuck. Out of work and Anna, not to mention Paula,
would give her hell. "Men. The bane of my existence. The
fuckers are nothing but trouble. Tall ones, short ones, fat
ones, old ones, and especially the young ones; nothing but

trouble, trouble, trouble and more trouble," she snarled at the elevator on its way to fetch her off the roof. A roof she wasn't likely to be allowed to enjoy. "Damn, damn, damn," she sighed, pressing her floor. Just to add a professional note to her last five minutes on the job, she changed into her black heels. And because it was a slow elevator, danced a few steps she and Shorty had been working on. Or were before the Lotus Room's unfortunate, ah, accident.

"Morning, Paula," Hackenbush said, passing the office manager.

"You're early, Mabel," Paula said handing her a cup of coffee.

"Thanks. I'm still figuring out the bus ecology so I gave myself too much time to get here," Hackenbush said. She shoved her bag under her temp assignment desk, hung her coat on her temp assignment coat-rack and turned on her temp assignment IBM compatible computer.

"Oh, well, you can meet Withers, Junior," Paula smiled at her. "And lucky," she lowered her voice, "he turned up this morning in a wonderful mood."

"Really?"

"Yes."

"Why'd'ya think that is?"

"Don't know, Mabel, he just looked happy when he got out of the elevator," Paula said.

"Really?"

"Yes." She glanced over her shoulder. "Here he comes, no swearing, okay?"

Mabel watched her long, tall elevator trouble stroll up the desk, never taking his amused gaze off her.

"Mr. Withers, this is Mabel Hackenbush, and–" Paula began.

"We met in the elevator. I believe this is yours, Ms Hackenbush," he said, handing her smoke to her.

"You're too kind," she said, watching him flick open a slim, gold lighter. "But do call me Hackenbush or Mabel, Mr. Withers, I like it so much better." She put the cigarette in her mouth and let him light it for her.

"I shall, very nice to meet you," Withers said, pocketing

his lighter, and left the scene.

"And what happened in the elevator, Hackenbush?" Paula asked

"I asked him for a light," Hackenbush said mysteriously from a cloud of smoke.

"And?"

"And, he said," she took another drag, "no."

Whatever Paula was going to say was interrupted by a phone that wouldn't stop ringing. She leaned over Hackenbush's desk to answer it. By the time she was done, Hackenbush was transcribing from the Dictaphone machine with such an innocent, but focused, look on her face; Paula decided she'd wait for a better moment to find out what else happened in the elevator. Or better, she'd have Bobby find out; Hackenbush liked him better anyway.

Withers Junior had a mirror in his office cunningly angled so he could keep an unobtrusive eye on his secretary. Usually he had better things to do and ignored whoever was out there, but Hackenbush was more interesting than anything on his desk at the moment. She was so focused on what she was doing, she seemed almost to be one with the Dictaphone. She also seemed to be able to smoke and drink coffee with hardly a ripple in her typing rhythm. And what posture; it would put a Sergeant-Major to shame. It had been her stance in the elevator that he remembered now; loosely coiled, but ready to spring nevertheless. The baggy coat had hidden a rather dowdy figure and the big black glasses had obscured a pair of bland brown eyes. He'd gotten a better look at those when he lit her cigarette. But none of that had much meaning when she moved, or even when she was still and about to move.

"I see you have another admirer here, Hackenbush," Withers Junior thought, watching Bobby Dreisler stop by her desk with coffee, a pack of cigarettes, a selection of donuts, more coffee, and then, apparently, just to worship her. Must have seemed that way to Paula, too, who chased him off every time she caught him there. Hackenbush kept her eyes to herself when Paula was on the rampage, but when they were alone, she smiled pleasantly at Bobby and listened, well, vivaciously, or so it seemed to Charles, who could not recall anyone listening to him like that lately (if ever). Curious beyond male endurance, Charles glided out of this office, past Hackenbush (who did not look up) and into the mailroom, where Bobby was diligently working away. "So, Bobby, how goes it here in the, ah, mailroom?"

Bobby could not really remember Withers Junior ever actually coming all the way into the mailroom and yet here he was leaning on the photocopier, seemingly parked there. It was a singular event, but Bobby, ever the aspiring hipster, did not lose his cool. "Very well, thank you, Mr. Withers," he said. He was well brought up, too.

"Just 'well'? We have such interesting people working here now," Charles said.

"Have we?"

"Yes, the new temp, what's her name?"

"Dr. Hackenbush?"

"She's a doctor? What kind of doc–"

"It's a joke, Charles," Frank said, joining the duo. "She's a musician. 'Dr. Hackenbush and her Orchestra'."

Bobby could count on one hand the times Withers Other had been in the mailroom. This was turning into an interesting morning. "She's a great musician," Bobby said. "And an inspiration to everyone."

"She is?" Charles asked, looking at Frank for clues as to why this might be so.

"Yes! She's astonishing and magical and lumen–"

"And both you Mr. Withers have calls waiting on your phones," Paula cut Bobby off mid-word from the doorway. "In your offices."

Withers Junior handed Bobby three twenties and told him to find out what everyone wanted for lunch. On his way back to his office, he noticed that Bobby started with Hackenbush's lunch order.

Hackenbush got off the bus at North Broadway and Johnston and just slumped for a moment. She wasn't the only one; several other mass transit riders were slumping along with her, waiting for the light to change. It had been a hellish bus ride—traffic, gridlock, traffic accidents, idiots in cars, idiots on foot—and she'd had to stand. Actually, what she didn't have to do was give her seat to an old woman, but, since she was betting on being an old woman someday, she figured she better store up all the good karma she could. "But I'd rather be dead than be on the bus at that age," she sighed.

Tired as she was, hunger got the better of her and she stopped for a half a chicken at Chapalita. Chapalita had ruined her for all other roasted chicken. Unfortunately they were sold out so she settled for two lingua tacos, one of which she ate on the way home. The bonus sandwich Withers Junior sprang for at lunch had been nice, but lunch was long ago and far away.

"Yes, lunch," she thought, walking home, eating her taco. Lunch had been the last normal moment of the day, which had descended into muted chaos with the arrival of Charles Withers, Senior, Esq. in his motorized wheelchair. His first action was to bump Hackenbush, who was innocently walking across the lobby, onto his lap and carry her off to his office.

Since she was on his lap she had a good, up-close look at him. He was older than God's wet nurse and had more wrinkles than anyone she'd ever seen alive. It was impressive, at least Mabel thought so, as she introduced herself.

"Ah, the new temp," he hissed, going around a corner on two wheels. "Fresh meat."

"Ah, too bad you've missed lunch, mister," she said. "That was all the fresh meat there was here."

He didn't laugh and wheeled her into his office, where he didn't protest when she got off his lap. "You're older than the last one," he growled, motoring up to his desk.

"Not really. I'm sure I'm only, oh, a fifth of your age."

"That would make you sixteen," he said, looking her over. "And if so, mam'selle, you're not holding up very well."

"Touché, dad," she thought, but merely smiled and said something about getting back to work. She was glad when he waved her off as he struck her as an angry, old guy and she wasn't in the mood to listen to any angry old guy bullsh–

"I see you met Withers Senior," Paula said, inspecting her for damage.

"Yes. And I was completely carried away by him. Ha. Ha ha. Ha." Hackenbush dragged the office manager into the mailroom. "So, like what, Paula, is the scoop on him and how often is he here?"

"He comes in when he feels up to it," Paula explained. "He comes in and the effort wears him out before he gets here and he gets really cranky when he's tired."

"Can we put him down for a nap? A little Seconal in his Bosco, maybe?"

"Very funny, Mabel, just remember; this guy is everybody's, including your, boss."

"El jefe. Le patron." Mabel saluted.

"Just steer clear of him, okay?"

"I'll try, but it was a sneak attack today."

"Watch your back. Especially the lower part."

"Yes, ma'am."

They went back to work. Sometime later they could hear Withers Senior yelling at Bobby. Paula told Mabel that was unusual because Bobby was his chief playmate. Bobby came out, red-faced, and shut himself up in the mailroom. Another kid, a tall, skinny redheaded one Hackenbush didn't know, went in and stayed there for a long time. There was no more yelling that afternoon, just ominous silence.

Hackenbush kept a low profile the rest of the day. Withers Junior had gone to a client meeting and Withers Other had gone to court so she had few distractions from her transcribing. She buzzed Bobby in the mailroom to see if he was okay and the poor kid sounded like he was almost in tears. She told him to buck up; it was only a day job. She thought she could hear him smile and would have gone in there and told him a joke or something if she hadn't felt like the hallway was 'mined' somehow. She left at the stroke of five, looking neither to the right, the left nor behind her as she went down the stairs (which were faster at rush hour).

And it seemed like the entire city was heading home at five that Friday.

So as she walked home eating one of her tacos, she wondered what nonsense Withers Senior was going to give her on this job. "And I thought Withers Junior was trouble. The only good Withers is the Withers Other," she thought, bolting the door behind her and leaning on it. Whatever it was, it would have to wait for Monday; she had a car-less weekend ahead of her, which did not mean she was excused from shopping and laundry and errands, alas. But the light was blinking on her answering machine and that always cheered her; someone somewhere wanted to talk to her and that could be nothing but wonderful. Yes, positive thinking could be applied to phone messages; too bad it was worthless everywhere else.

It was Bruno Carlos with a pretty standard song list: *Wave, Meditation, Night and Day, One Note Samba, The Coffee Song, Estrada Branca, Lady Be Good* (Hackenbush could have done without the wheezy leer behind that title, but, oh well), *Stardust* (with a Brazilian beat? Well, let's try it. If anyone could carry it off, it was Hackenbush and Carlos), *I Won't Dance, Day In, Day Out, When Your Lover Has Gone* ("Ah, now there's a great song" she thought). He named a tune she'd never heard of - *The Goodbye Look*. And then the message ran out and she was reaching for the phone to call Tim at Rockaway Records, to find out what the fuck *The Goodbye Look* was, when the message beeped at her and it was Carlos playing the record for her. Much to her horror, after the synthesized steel drum intro, Donald Fagen of Steely Dan (or formerly of Steely Dan, she supposed) was singing at her and doing a fairly impressive job. Her message was only a minute long, so Carlos kept calling back and dropping the needle more or less where he'd left off. As neurotic as this way of leaning a song was, Hackenbush had a fairly good idea of the tune and what she could do to, ah, with it.

Nothing against Mr. Fagen or his song; her problem was more with Carlos, who always seemed to find a song that upset Hackenbush's theory that no song of any value had been composed after 1964. It was a cozy assumption for her; it kept her warm at night and singing material that could be Hackenbushed and still hold up. Tough songs like *You Go To*

My Head, A Fine Romance; brutes of songs like *Body And Soul* and *Stardust*; songs that almost sang the singer and usually mauled a lesser musician than Hackenbush. And even she never claimed to have mastered any of these songs because she always found something new in them. Or perhaps they found something new in her as she aged. Too bad she didn't have time to dwell on that comforting thought; she filed it away for when she needed something to keep her going.

She played Carlos' messages again, mildly impressed by the melody and really digging what she could hear of the guitar player. Nice groove, AABABBAB structure; definitely a Hackenbushable tune and wasn't it odd that she and Donald Fagen sang in the same key? "I wonder which one of us should be alarmed by that?" she asked herself

In addition to Carlos, Shorty called to say he'd be there a week from Sa'day; Luis Taylor, Carlos' bass player, called to say he'd give her a ride to and from the gig (he lived up in Highland Park so they were almost neighbors); and then Shorty called again to ask her when and where they could rehearse their dancing for Sa'day. She made a mental note to call these guys back and then called Tim, at Rockaway.

The store was blaring the new Little Feat single (which, Hackenbush supposed, rocked in a mindless kind of way, if you like that sort of thing), and yelled that she'd like to talk to Tim, please. He came on the phone and she yelled that she needed the lyrics off a song called *The Goodbye Look* by Donald Fagen, could he pretty please help her out and she'd be much obliged? He said okay and put the phone down, cruelly not putting her on hold so she had to listen to more Little Feat, the next song being far inferior to the hit single, which even Hackenbush had heard somewhe–

"Got it," Tim said and read it to her as she jotted it down. "You singing this somewhere?"

She told him the Island Room, 9 PM, Sa'day, sorry, Saturday the twentieth. He said he'd be there and he'd tell people and she didn't doubt it; Tim was one of her more loyal fans.

"You're my hero, dahlin'," she drawled and hung up, wondering for the nth time why she couldn't hook up with a nice, normal, steadily employed guy like Tim. And for the nth time she shrugged, reminding herself Tim and his kind were all happily married to females very unlike Hackenbush. The Tims of this world were easy-going guys married to easy going gals, which is why they were all easy-going. "Oh well," she said and realized she hadn't sat down since leaving the office, almost three hours ago. So she sat on her couch and ate the other taco, which was good even cold.

It would have been a luxury to take a hot shower and go to bed, but she had too much to do. She went over Carlos' song list in her head while she smoked a cigarette. Then she stood up, sang a few scales and sang through the more predictable songs, songs that she'd sing more or less as is so the guys could solo. There might be a fillip or two on her last chorus out, but not much. She then tackled the tougher songs—*Stardust*, *I Won't Dance*, *Lady Be Good*—songs that were easy to do wrong and that could go very wrong with an unpredictable guy like Carlos.

Hackenbush had worked with Carlos and Luis enough to know that whatever weird conga thing Carlos might do, Luis would keep them all out of hell with his bass. Luis was a wonderful bass player; he was everywhere a band ever needed him to be. Most bands, the good ones, always gave him room to shine on his own and shine he did. It wasn't that Carlos' band was bad, it was Carlos' leadership that suffered when he got carried away with a song.

So she rehearsed by herself, trying to hear Carlos' congas in her head, she wound up listening to Luis' bass more and more. She wondered who he had on guitar and drums; if they were good, it would be a good night. If they were flakes or prima donnas, she and Luis would have their hands full keeping the music going over the egos.

But she'd worry about that next week. Right now she was in deep communion with *Stardust*, dragging the vowels over a syncopated rhythm and crashing the consonants over the bar lines, until it wasn't so much a song anymore as a happy howl all through the resonating chambers of her body. It was the physical act of singing, the roar from head to toe that she let herself go in for a while. She bent at the waist to let the high notes loose in her head and blood rush up and drive out the day, the worry, the troubles, and the nicotine. She let the song run loose with her and began to rein them both back down to earth or at least back into the stratosphere. Eyes closed, swaying, almost back in a civilized groove, she reached for where her baritone ukulele would have been... if she still had one.

"Damn!" she barked, shaking her empty fist at nothing. She slammed her palm on the closed piano and listened to the strings growl at her.

"Fuck with me, will you?" she thought, opening the one instrument she did have and played a few bars of *Lady Be Good*. She began to sing, decided she was rushing, and started again a hair slower. She elongated the phrases so there were no breaks in the melody, one long tone with hills and valleys. On the second chorus, she picked up the tempo and subjected it some glottal machine gun phrasing, ignoring the vowels completely. She tried to fit it into what she thought Carlos might give her as a conga line, but kept hearing tiki room music and sound effects and gave it up as a bad job. She had to stop to laugh at a memory of listening to one of her father's old records from the sixties—*The Polynesia Room Jazz Quartet*—she recalled her clarinet-playing father in his Hawaiian shirt and grousing that woodwinds would never stand up in the humidity of the islands; however and nevertheless, a gig's a gig.

"Yeah, a gig's a gig and I got one a week from Sa'day," she told her upright and dug out a fake book for the changes on *I Won't Dance*. Like most of Kern, she liked the lyrics better than the melody, but was stuck with both. She sang it straight a few times and decided she used all the inspiration she had for that evening on *Stardust* and *Lady Be Good*. She also knew this was bullshit, but it gave her an excuse to play Carlos' phone messages with *The Goodbye Look* on them and work on that.

"Ah, progress," she thought trying to pull the song inside out to see what it was made of. She copped the copa rhythm and picked up the chord changes; mostly, Hackenbush never claimed to be a great pianist or even a good one. And this would have all been easier if she'd had a baritone uke to work with. But if she had a baritone uke to work with, she wouldn't have this gig with Carlos. Oh well, never mind, we must solo on what God gives us to solo on, even when it's crap.

She played and sang until about midnight; even gave *I Won't Dance* another tumble and felt better about it afterwards. At least Carlos hadn't put *Body And Soul* on the list; it was her nemesis and she needed more strength than she had just then to scuffle with it. She sang the first verse and felt used and unworthy, and then realized she was just tired and it was late. She smoked one last cigarette and went to bed.

The next morning, Hackenbush faced simple errands in LA without a car. More complex errands might involve a messenger service or a fax machine or a taxi or even the extreme of renting a car. But simple errands were challenging enough and over her morning coffee and that first, inspirational cigarette, Mabel was contemplating her strategy like a general before a battle.

"Laundry, grocery shopping and return library books," she thought, considering the distances involved. She could do her laundry in the place next to Rocky's Pizza on Eastlake or a half-block away on the south side of North Broadway next to the Roberto's Mexican restaurant. The one on North Broadway had a TV, which could be a plus or minus, but was not crucial, since she had a new issue of "The Economist" magazine to read, and songs to redesign in her head if "The Economist" pissed her off too much.

Her shopping choices were more limited. If she had her car, she'd go to the Highland Park Luckys or the Vons in South Pasadena, depending on how fragile she was feeling. Grocery stores threw her into a major funk; she could never think of anything to buy once she got in there, and usually clipped coupons just for a few ideas. But those luxury days were over; she knew she'd have to start packing a lunch on Monday to economize because cute as he was, Withers Junior was not always going to spring for lunch.

"He is cute," she said, trying out her voice for the first time that day. "In a tall, dark and handsome way."

But back to shopping: her walking distance choices were Safeway over on Daly (big, glaringly lit and grubby) or Big Saver down the street (small, dim and grubby). There was another market on Griffin and North Broadway, but the one time she'd tried it, she found her LA restaurant Spanish simply wasn't up to it.

The library books were really the biggest issue on her list. She couldn't renew over the phone and she was such a girl scout at heart and cheap, the thought of overdue fines was just more than she could stand. The local branch was closed for earthquake repairs that were never begun because the city would rather tear it down and build a new one, but the community loved its funky deco lines so much that Hackenbush had signed a petition and even gone to a meeting downtown to save it. And save it they did and there it was— closed in all its deco glory. So her options were: use two of her precious bus tickets and schlep them either to the Highland Park regional branch on North Figueroa Avenue, which would send them back to the temporary main branch where she originally got them, or actually go to the temporary main branch, since the original one, which was on Flower Street, was still closed after a fire. She looked at the four mysteries she'd thoroughly enjoyed and thought, "I hope you're worth it, Messrs. Wolfe and Marlowe because...wait a sec, I seem to recall..." Digging out the white pages, she found that, yes, there was a tiny library in Lafayette Park, which was waking distance from the office. She could return them there and they'd get the books back downtown. She could even send Bobby to return her books; he'd love to do something like that for her.

"Poor kid. Wonder what was bothering him on Friday," Mabel thought, changing from her robe to a long, baggy walking dress, tights and her tennis shoes. Her first stop was at the Superior Mercado where she bought an extremely unfashionable, but very useful wire basket with wheels. She'd rather look bad than rip up the rotator cuffs in her shoulders carrying heavy bags. She took it for a test drive through Big

Saver and either they'd spruced the joint up since her last visit or she'd sadly misjudged it; she found it better lit and less grimy than she remembered it. This cut her supermarket funk in half and she prowled the aisles and bought sack lunch materials: apples, saltines, peanut butter, pita bread, fruit chews, and cashews. She picked up a carton of Pall Malls, half and half, coffee and ramen noodles, which would keep her going until she could dream up a more interesting grocery list.

On her way home, Hackenbush resisted the urge to buy a chicken at Chapalita and ate one of the apples instead. Dragging the cart behind her wasn't terrible, one of the elderly señoras even complimented her on it, so that was all to the good. Chez Hackenbush, she unloaded her cart and put her laundry sack, magazine and soap in it. She bumped her chariot down the stairs and decided to go to the Eastlake Laundromat. She could get a slice of pizza at Rocky's, which delivered, or fish from the Mercado del Mar in the same mini mall. Ceviche for lunch might be just the thing.

So she towed her cart and smiled and nodded at the neighbors who made eye contact and ignored the ones who did not. Most did; Hackenbush had lived there long enough to be considered the loco, but harmless middle-aged gringa who kept late hours. She returned the nod of one of the Eastlake boys whose face was bruised up and, being an east side person, she wondered if and how much the gang territories had shifted last night.

The laundry was busy, but she got a washer right away. She settled on a plastic chair and regretfully told an older lady who wanted to chat with her that she didn't speak Spanish. Mabel had enough Spanish to tell her this and apologize in Spanish, which might have been confusing, except it happened all the time in LA, in all kinds of languages. So they just smiled at each other; Mabel read her magazine and the señora found someone else to chat with.

After shifting her stuff to the dryers, her stomach growled at her. Mabel took a few quarters and went to the bakery next door and got the smallest pain dolce they had. She didn't particularly like Mexican sweet bread, but this rough mildly sweet loaf really hit the spot just then.

She folded her laundry, one of the teenage girls did the sheet dance with her—there were no men in the Laundromat that day—and packed up her cart. She got a small order of ceviche and went home. At home she put the laundry away and ate her lunch and was pleased that she was right on schedule—she'd planned to start working at 1:00 and it was only 12:45—she could even smoke a cigarette in peace.

She went over Carlos' song list and didn't have any new insights into it, so she left it alone. Besides, Shorty was coming over at four o'clock to work out the dances for that gig and he usually had some interesting new ideas. Not always useful ideas, but usually good for a few laughs at least. That was one of the reasons she kept him around; he was reliable, amusing and light on his feet.

So, instead, Hackenbush pulled out the charts she was working on for her band. She had rearranged *You Go To My Head* and *Stormy Weather* almost beyond recognition, but they needed it. In fact; they were asking for it, and Hackenbush was just the girl to do it to them.

You Go To My Head ended up syncopated beyond recognition except for the lyrics, but *Stormy Weather* was a trickier proposition. Due to the extreme suffering in the lyrics, the song had almost a mystical following and her rendition would piss off quite a few people. Well, they could all go to hell. Her version was up tempo, swung hard and wide, and marched its brokenhearted lyrics into the horizon. "Suffering," she thought. "I have sung to you of my suffering and now I must go. I'm double parked anyway."

She lifted her pen off the guitar part to wipe the nib and think about her guitar player, Gregg Miller. He was barely twenty-five, a kid, something of a punk kid, but with great technique and instincts that might, provided with the right stimulus, turn into great sensibilities. 'Provided he doesn't get his heart smashed up or drink too much,' she thought, ticking off all the fine musicians who didn't last for one reason or another.

Like Paula Dreisler. Well, poor lady, it was like Anna Kodaly said, Paula had a kid to raise and never asked for her husband to die in a car accident. He'd been a great bass player, too.

Men, y'just can't depend on 'em fer nuthin'.

And it's a myth that you can sing on a broken heart. Maybe later, when you've healed a little, but not right away. Maybe never, like Paula.

Oh, fuck the past, all of it.

So she thought about Gregg Miller instead. He was cute, it was a fact, and not an unpleasant one. And if she had to look at someone during his solo, well, it helped if he was easy on the eyes. He was a good guitar player, getting on to wonderful as he got to know her singing better and know to stay the hell out of her way when she was singing. He was an edgier and harder player than most jazz guys around town because he'd played in punk and rock bands until he got bored. He'd gone to the Guitar Institute of Technology and learned what little they could teach him there and then played in various bands in town for a few years. Then he truly lucked out when Hackenbush's previous guitar player moved to Vegas ("Steady money gigs in Vegas," he'd said and that was the last she ever heard of him, so it must be so) and Gregg had impressed her with his lanky bad boy charm and even more with his hipster licks.

Impressed her, Cody, the bass player, Ross, the drummer and Shorty, the dance partner enough to give him a go. He was young and brash and although he had cooled it with hitting on her, he hadn't really stopped flirting with her. She'd managed not to laugh in his face because that would be too mean, but had let him know very clearly that she found him more amusing than arousing.

She knew Cody and Ross tolerated Gregg off the stand and dug him on it. They'd been with Hackenbush for a long time, they knew she was tough on guitar players, they told her this one might live up to all their standards because he was consistently good, and great oftener and oftener. She further knew that Shorty had a big crush on the kid, and that Gregg was the only one in the dark about it. Ah well, as long as they could make music together, who cared who loved whom or how or how well?

She made some notes in the margin of a copy of *The Song Is You* as she hummed through the bridge and didn't find anything to hook onto there. Nevertheless, she had her suspicions that there was something nice lurking in the tune and decided to come back to it later. Maybe she'd go to Rockaway and see if they had any used LPs with it on them. "Yeah, just hop over to Rockaway," she frowned, remembering she didn't have a car and Rockaway was far, far away...on the bus. "Just hop on over there...on my broom."

And it would have to wait anyway because she didn't have any spare cash at the moment. Ugh. She turned on her record player and danced around the couch to Django Reinhart's *Swing from Paris*. It made her feel better and she needed to warm up for Shorty anyway.

Somewhere over the din of her heels on the hardwood and the dead gypsy's guitar riffs, she heard Shorty's scooter pull up on the porch. "Hi you," she said, leaning out the window, watching him chain up his Vespa. Hey, hey, it was more transportation than Hackenbush had at the moment.

"Howz yer day, Mabel?" Shorty asked on his way in.

"Oh fine. Most productive, domestically and artistically. D'you want some fruit chews and vodka or shall we break out the gin and the blender?" she asked.

"Oh, gin fizzes. I need the protein."

Hackenbush put together the ice, the gin, the sugar, the half and half, the lemon and lime juice and vanilla together in the blender while Shorty separated the white from the yolk.

"Got any Triple Sec?" Shorty asked.

Hackenbush waved an almost new bottle of orange flower water at him and asked him what kind of a savage he thought she was. "I must have used up my last bit of luck getting this," she told him, carefully doling out two drops. "Contact," she said and watched him fire up the blender.

They drank in silence for a while. At least half of a good gin fizz should be enjoyed in silence so one can fully appreciate the melange of flavors and let the gin creep as only gin can.

"How are you, Hackenbush?" Shorty asked over his half-finished drink.

Ginger Mayerson

"Tired, but I've got a good paying, steady money temp job," she said, licking her lips. "So I'm on the road to financial recovery. I can be tired for a few weeks if it gets me the car fixed, a new uke, and God willing, Tanaka will have us back at the Lotus Room."

"I saw Wang last night," Shorty said. "He's bartending at the Osaka Club until the Lotus Room is fixed up."

"He must hate it," Hackenbush said. She and the band had played there, it was a barn of a place, noisy and freezing. The rangy angles of the Lotus Room were positively cozy compared to the Osaka Club.

"He does; he misses us," Shorty told her. "He said Mr. Tanaka is still mad at you, but is beginning to see that it wasn't really your fault."

"Oh yeah?"

"Yeah, Wang said Mr. Tanaka is also beginning to see that the insurance money will put the Lotus Room back together again."

"It was a nice room, wasn't it?"

"Wasn't it ever? So, Mr. Tanaka might, given a little more time, might be able to remember how much he likes you again," Shorty finished up.

"Wang is working on this, isn't he?"

"Uh huh."

"And whatever Wang wants, Wang gets." Hackenbush finished her drink. "This gives me courage."

"Yeah, that orange flower water really makes a difference," Shorty said.

"Not the drink, Shorty. Wang; Wang on our side; the love of our good Wang," she said. "Wang gives me courage."

"Oh, yeah, right. So what's up for Sa'day and Carlos?"
She told him.

"I dunno about this *Goodbye Look*," Shorty said over the rim of his glass.

"I believe it has much potential," Hackenbush said, clicking the metronome on and singing the first verse to him.

Being smart and talented, Shorty picked up the rhythm and they were dancing in no time. Occasionally he stopped to work something out, but mostly he just called out directions as

38

they danced. He and Hackenbush had been dancing for years, so they had a lot of telepathy going on already. "Needs work, Mabel," Shorty told her on a break. "But, yes, has potential. Also needs a rehearsal with Carlos so we know what he wants from this tune; can you get to one this week?"

"I have been thinking we can use the roof at work one or two lunch hours," she said, pouring them both cranberry juices. "Whaddya think?"

"I think that's fine if it don't get you fired."

"Oh, I think I can work it out." Hackenbush set her drink down. "What now?"

"I had some new ideas for *Lady Be Good*."

They danced, incorporating new steps into old routines. Most of Carlos' list was songs they had been performing for years so it was no great hardship to do them again.

Shorty stayed for dinner, which was another round of gin fizzes, and then went on his way. He was a career house-sitter and had a settled place for the next few months. When he was between house-sitting gigs, he stayed with Hackenbush or at any number of other hospitable friends' places. He was fun to have around, for a few days at least, and never overstayed his welcome.

So after he left, Hackenbush washed her blender and tidied up the kitchen. She felt mentally restless, but physically tired so she put on one of her many Billie Holliday records and listened rather impatiently through *Some Other Spring*, which was a great tune and on the Hackenbush "to do someday" list. And then *Ghosts Of Yesterday*, which was nowhere near the "to do someday" list, but not on the "I'll see you in hell first" list. And then relaxed into the first bars of *Body And Soul*. It was better than a gin fizz for putting the world right, no matter how wrong it all might be.

And on Sunday, she rested.

With a better feel for the buses of Los Angeles, Hackenbush was able to get to work only fifteen minutes early. That was fine with her; she hated to rush and fifteen minutes early was impressively conscientious without being annoying and compulsive. So she flung Paula a showgirl smile and got a cup of coffee. She found it odd that a case of sugar packets rained down from the cabinet above the coffee maker, but, hey, possibly seismic activity had shifted the contents of that cabinet just so. Or it was gremlins; yes, that side of Westlake was crawling with gremlins. Who knew? With Adela's help, Hackenbush scooped all the packets back in the box and shoved it firmly well back on its shelf. She thanked the blonde-at-the-roots-(for a change)-blonde and headed for her secretarial alcove. Dropping her overstuffed tote bag on her stenographer chair, she took a startled step back as the chair fell apart under the bag.

"Hmmmmmm, even paranoids have enemies, however..." she said. "Ahm, Paula, have you got a Phillips head screwdriver I could use?"

Bobby turned up a few seconds later, frowned at the disassembled chair and went to get a screwdriver.

By the time he got back, Hackenbush was perusing the Help menu on her computer, trying to find out how to get back to the Western alphabet from the, she presumed, Greek or Russian character set now on her screen. Good thing she was able to read and follow directions because Bobby didn't know how to change it and Paula had the tall, skinny redheaded file clerk cornered, grilling him as to what other little "improvements" Withers Senior had had made to the office for Hackenbush. It was an interrogation in vain because Paula couldn't do anything rash, like fire the punk, without Withers Senior's okay and Withers Senior wasn't about to lose his new henchman now that Bobby was on strike from that position and the punk knew it. He acted innocent and just this side of insolent.

So there was nothing to be done, but be careful and let Bobby decommission all the traps he thought might be set around the office. He should know; he used to be the chief trap setter. Hackenbush carefully went though her desk area and only found two pens broken so the ink would get all over everything and a pot of glue set to spill into her printer. Paula looked over the ladies room and called Maintenance to screw the toilet seats back down.

It was when the filing cabinet that was set to fall on Hackenbush fell on Bobby, just grazing his leg (but it could have just as well broken it), that Hackenbush took Paula aside. "Paula, my dear, is this the normal temp hazing or something special?" she asked.

"Oh, this is special and just for you," Paula said. "And I'm afraid it's only the beginning."

"Me, too, and I need this gig," Mabel said seriously. "So, am I wrong or does Withers Senior have too much free time and no one to occupy him?"

"That's accurate if you leave out that he's a mean old bastard, yes."

"Really, Paula, I couldn't care less," Hackenbush said loftily. "I'm interested in solving the problem more than his failings as a human being."

"A solution? Do tell!"

"Hire him an assistant."

"Hackenbush, you've no idea how many assistants have limped out of here."

"Not just any assistant," Hackenbush cut her off. "Someone who can handle a guy with a big ego and an even bigger contempt for all humanity. Someone who's worked with..." Hackenbush lowered her voice, looked left and then right. "Ballet choreographers."

"No!"

"Yassss!"

"And who would this wonder be?" Paula asked.

"Suzy Reed."

"She'd never come here," Paula scoffed. "She's dancing all over the country; steady money, I heard."

"Old news, Paula, old news; Suzy is in the middle of an existential crisis and turning forty very soon, if you must know," Hackenbush said. "She's wondering if she even wants to dance anymore, it's such a burn-out field. She's vulnerable. She's temp secretary material if I ever saw it."

"Is that so? How can we get her?"

"Anna Kodaly." Hackenbush picked up the phone and handed it to Paula. "Tell Anna to tell Suzy that two vocalists are in a jam and Suzy, and only Suzy, can bail us out. This will reaffirm the natural order of dancer superiority over vocalists once more and will inspire the right amount of pity in La Suzy so that–"

"Hush!" Paula hissed at her and walked away with the phone to beg Anna for help in private.

Hackenbush swirled her cool, or what was left of it, around her and strolled back to her desk. On the way she nearly collided with Withers Junior "Oh, hello dere."

"I understand you've been having an, um, interesting morning," he said sympathetically.

"All mornings are interesting in the legal profession, don't you think, Mr. Withers?" she drawled.

"Why, yes," he said, trying and failing to determine based on the look in her eye if she was kidding him. "Yes, of course they are. You haven't been too bruised up by your interesting morning have you, Miss, ah, Dr. Hackenbush?"

"No, but Bobby caught a filing cabinet in the leg a while ago," she said seriously.

"Yes, that's who I've just been talking to–"

"Excuse me." Seeing the front part of a wheelchair emerging from the elevator, Hackenbush slid behind a large potted plant until Withers Senior had roared by and into his office. "Your father," she said, parting the fronds. "He's a kind of spry and feisty old guy, isn't he?"

Withers Junior wondered for a moment if the words "spry" and "feisty" had developed some new meaning he didn't know about and then said, "Yes, he is," and fled into his office.

Hackenbush went back to her alcove and sat at her desk. She moved a few things around and then decided to have a chat with Bobby. But not Bobby-the-mailroom-guy, she needed Bobby-the-guitar-player-guy. However, she found him in the mailroom. "Hi."

"Hi."

"How's the leg?"

"Okay."

"Ahm, listen kid, keep this to yourself, but if I can arrange it, a couple of people are coming this week to rehearse some stuff with me on the roof," she said leaning in and whispering conspiratorially. "We could use a guitar player up there and you're the only one in the building I know about, whaddya say?"

"Me?"

"You!" She winked at him. "The song in question is called *The Goodbye Look*." She gave him the run down on the composer and the album and sang a few bars. He told her he'd "work it out" and she said, "Good man. I'll let you know the day and time." She smiled and extended the bundle of Chandlers and Stouts. "Oh, and by the way, could you drop these books at the Lafayette Park Library for me?"

Bobby blushed, took the mysteries and looked up at her. "Hackenbush, I...I–"

"Oh, there you are, Mabel," Paula rushed in. "Good news!"

"Suzy is willing to condescend–?"

"A job's a job, Hackenbush, and this is a good one for her," Paula said sharply. "At least we hope so. She'll be here at one."

"We must also hope it's a good job for us or we'll have to shoot the old boy with the tranquilizer gun or something. Eh, Bobby?"

Bobby smiled at her and then Withers Junior buzzed him to come into his office to get money and get lunch for everyone.

"Get La Suzy a tuna sandwich on a French or Kaiser roll, no cheese, no extra mayo and lots of sprouts," Hackenbush told him. "La Suzy likes sprouts."

"Dancers." Paula rolled her eyes in unison with Hackenbush.

Bobby, who didn't know who La Suzy was or anything about dancers, just looked puzzled and went off to get lunch for everyone. He took Hackenbush's books to the library first.

Hackenbush was just lighting up her after-luncheon cigarette when La Suzy arrived. She peeked around the corner as the tall, lean, ash blonde glided over to the reception desk and asked for Paula. The dancer was wearing a gray wool suit with the skirt cut above mid-thigh (quite original in these days of calf-length, drop-waist baggy dresses), and her long, powerful legs were encased in woolly tights. She was wearing flats, but her calf muscles were bulging as if she were wearing high heels; it was their natural state.

"If I had legs like that, I could take over the world," Hackenbush thought, leaning back so Suzy wouldn't catch her spying on her. Suzy Reed fascinated Hackenbush; if she could have an older sister, it would be Suzy, but since she didn't have an older sister, she was happy to be tolerated by Suzy whenever they met. Suzy was six feet, three inches tall on point and too curvy for the big-time ballet world. She had considered having a breast reduction, but because she couldn't get a height reduction, she decided not to mutilate her body for nothing. Therefore, she'd carved out a niche in the minimal Los Angeles dance scene as a powerful modern dancer with a classical attitude. It was intense, but it worked, and Suzy had as much dancing as she wanted for many years. But all good things come to an end. Or possibly Suzy just got tired of being brilliant for the thirty dedicated serious dance fans in LA. And there wasn't much production money around, less than usual, as it seemed like all the art money in town was going to build buildings for art instead of funding the creation of art for the buildings LA already had. Of course, a concert hall is easy to understand and most modern dance is not.

Suzy could type a little, add and subtract, answer phones, and get coffee pleasantly as anyone, possibly more so, and that's what she was doing that winter. Of course working in offices is easier to understand than why the dance steps still haunted her feet, but not her heart. She winked at Hackenbush without breaking her regal stride as she was escorted down the hall to Paula's office. A moment later Paula buzzed Hackenbush to come in there, too.

"Hullo, Suzy, glad you could make it." Hackenbush slid into a chair in front of Paula's desk and next to Suzy.

"Glad to be here, Mabel. Anna says this is a madhouse," Suzy drawled. "You must fit right in."

"Oh yes! And the coffee is good, too." Hackenbush rolled her eyes at Paula.

"Seriously, ladies, what's the deal?" Suzy asked, cutting

right to the chase.

"Our most senior partner needs an assistant," Paula said. "He's in his eighties, confined to a wheelchair, and doesn't practice much law anymore, but he does need someone to carry files and get coffee and–"

"And keep him from terrorizing the office," Hackenbush said bluntly. "He's bored, he needs someone to focus his extra energy on, someone to pay attention to him, someone–"

"I was getting to all that, Hackenbush," Paula snarled.

"Well, you weren't getting there fast enough," Mabel snarled back. "Suzy, we need you. We need you to keep this guy in line with your charm, your tact and your strong muscles, if need be. And out of the office, if possible. I think you'll be able to wrap this old codger around your little finger in five minutes, so this job will be a cakewalk."

"And if I can't wrap him around my finger?" Suzy asked, amused by Hackenbush's impassioned plea.

"Then we're both out of work because I can't cope with flying file cabinets any better than the seven temps that were here before me," Hackenbush said, staring straight into the dancer's eyes. She felt more than heard Paula groan.

"What the fu–" Suzy began.

"Okay, here's the unvarnished story on this joint." Hackenbush told her everything Anna had said about Withers and Sons and everything that had happened since she'd met Withers Senior "Anna didn't tell you all this?" Hackenbush asked at the end of her recital.

"Yes, but I didn't believe it," Suzy said, looking from one singer to the other.

"What do you think, Suzy? Will you give it a try?" Paula asked.

"I'm not a baby-sitter."

"This is more diplomacy than diapering, Suzy," Paula said.

"Yeah, what she said," Hackenbush added rather pointlessly.

"Well, can't hurt to meet him," Suzy said after she'd thought it over for a minute. A job's a job and this one paid well, enough to take a serious look at it before she rejected it out of hand.

They all stood up and since Hackenbush only came up to Suzy's shoulder, the dancer looked down at her and said she thought she was looking well.

Hackenbush thanked her and went back to her desk. She watched Paula usher Suzy into Withers Senior's office and come out a few seconds later and close the door. "Hey!" she hissed at her sister vocalist.

"What?" Paula hissed back.

"You're leaving her alone in there? With HIM?"

"I think she can handle it."

"I certainly hope so."

They both jumped when Charles hissed, "Why are we whispering?" They had not seen him come up to Hackenbush's desk. "Will you photocopy these, Mabel? I've got the client waiting in my office." He walked away.

"Sure," Mabel growled and went into the mailroom to photocopy.

"Hey, who was that?" Bobby asked, breaking off his conversation with the redheaded file clerk.

"Who?"

"That tall blonde that came in after lunch."

"That's Suzy Reed, you know, you got her a sandwich today." Hackenbush stuck another stack of paper in the feeder.

"Oh yeah? I put her sandwich in the fridge."

"Well, that's good," Hackenbush said as she cleared a paper jam. "You wouldn't want to poison her on her first day, would you?"

"That's not what I'd want to do with her," the redheaded kid said.

"Oh yeah? Well, maybe you can take a break from your sick fantasies and fix this copier," Mabel snapped, banging the copier door against the wall. "C'mon, guys, get useful."

There was no arguing with a pissed off Hackenbush; Bobby knew this already and the redhead was a quick learner, so they fixed the copier and finished the job for her. She tossed a "Thanks" over her shoulder as she left. Knocking before entering, she took the originals and the copies into Charles's office and gave them to the guys in boring suits sitting in there. They said thanks and she left them to whatever legal stuff they were doing. A partnership, she surmised based on the documents she'd gotten ready for this meeting. She gave a worried glance at Withers Senior's still closed door and found Paula at her desk, also watching it. "Good view from here." Mabel offered her a cigarette and they both lit up.

They were still silently smoking when Suzy opened Withers Senior's door and then pushed him out in a lightweight wheelchair. The lawyer muttered something about errands and asked Paula to call his driver, even added a "Please" to it.

While Paula was on the phone, Mabel made eye contact with Withers Other, who'd come to see whom his father was saying 'please' to; it was such an unusual occurrence. Charles stepped out of his office with more copying for Hackenbush and was blocked by his father's unmotorized wheelchair, which he simply stared at.

"Your driver will meet you both in the parking garage, Mr. Withers," Paula said breaking the spell.

"Excellent! If you would please be so kind, Suzanne," Withers Senior said and away they went.

Charles snapped out of it and asked Hackenbush to make copies. She did, and when she got back, Frank was leaning on her desk.

"I haven't seen my father in that wheelchair in a long time," he said.

"No? Hold on a sec." Hackenbush darted into Charles's office and gave him the copies and the originals. "What about it?" she asked when she got back to Frank.

"He usually doesn't put himself in anybody's power like that," Frank told her.

"That don't surprise me."

"So, who was that?"

"Suzy Reed, his new assistant, I presume he's in her power, as you say." Hackenbush lit a cigarette and pinched a piece of tobacco off her tongue. She smiled at Adela coming down the hallway.

"I think I need an assistant," Frank muttered.

"No you don't," Adela said, handing him a stack of papers and herding him back into his office.

Hackenbush exhaled a lungful of smoke and went back to work, which included setting up the rehearsal for Thursday.

As Paula had warned her, the office was either mellow or go-like-hell. Withers' deal had gone into high gear the day before and at seven o'clock that Tuesday evening Hackenbush had hours of work ahead of her. She frowned and buzzed Paula. "I don't mind staying and doing this," she told the office manager. "Overtime is a wonderful thing. Unfortunately, walking home from the bus stop at eleven or midnight is scary even for me."

"We have taxi vouchers," Paula said, busy with her own work.

"Then I'm your girl."

"Good."

At eight, Withers came out of his office, looking lovely, and apologized to Hackenbush. "If I could get out of this party I would stay and work with you guys, but I can't," he said, adjusting his overcoat.

"How terrible you have to party when you'd rather be here, slaving away." Hackenbush leaned forward so he could light her cigarette. Quick with that lighter, he was.

"Yes, well, some things must simply be endured." He waved to a very pretty young woman and introduced her to Mabel as Belinda Rafeson. He seemed awfully glad to see the slim, washed-out blonde and that annoyed Hackenbush more than she wanted to admit. "Looks like a tall drink of water, as they say," she thought, and then added: "Of course not everyone can be a glamorous, overworked brunette."

Frank came up to the little group, said hello to the colorless Belinda and asked her how she was. Mabel decided this was a good time to put the headphones back on and type like a madwoman. Out of her peripheral vision she saw Charles and Belinda leave and Frank linger. She ignored him, hoping he'd go away. He did not; he simply shifted to the chair by her desk. She continued to type, but could hear him over the tape.

"Everyone assumes they'll get married," he said. "I suppose that would be okay, if she and I weren't in love."

Hackenbush typed faster and even closed her eyes. "Love," she mentally spat. "All love does is fuck your head up." The tape ended and when she opened her eyes, she found Frank had gone and her left hand had shifted over one key to the right. She cursed, deleted that text and backed the tape up, wondering why the hell people tell temps things they wouldn't tell their doctor, their lawyer, their best friend? Why?

At nine, Paula came by with a taxi voucher and a key. "Lock up when you leave," she said.

"Is Frank gone?" Hackenbush asked, stubbing out a cigarette she hadn't really wanted in the first place.

"Yup, you're on your own now," Paula said. "Be good," she tossed over her shoulder on her way out.

Hearing the door click closed, Hackenbush gave in to a nutty urge to kick off her shoes and run up and down the hall and around the back office. She did a few hops for good measure. As she was doing a war dance back to her alcove, she discovered the cleaning crew guys were her audience. "Hola," she said politely.

"Buenos tardes, señorita," they said and started vacuuming to save her any further embarrassment.

She was deeply impressed by their cool. "I bet they see that sort of thing all the time," she thought. "At least I was dressed."

At half past ten, she called it a night, called a cab and went down to the lobby to wait for it. "Hi there, my name is Mabel," she said tiredly to the security guy there.

"My name Walter."

"Nicetameetcha. Is it always this dark down here?"

"Conserving energy, miss."

"Ah," she said. "I'll just go pace over there then." She moved off to a shadowy part of the lobby. If she had to wait, she might as well practice the steps she and Shorty had worked on over the weekend. She sang *Lady Be Good* in a low voice and danced with care and precision. She was so wrapped up in what she was doing, she didn't see the guy's legs until she tripped over them and woke him up. "Sorry, mister," she said backing away from the raggedy figure.

He just grunted and curled back into the wall.

"Enjoyed your show, lady."

Hackenbush swung round and found she had a small audience of tired-looking men and women. "Oh, thanks," she said, and bowed for the smattering of applause. "Ahhhh...um, come here often?" she asked.

"Only when it gets below a certain temperature," Walter said, materializing beside her and leading her back to his desk by the front doors.

"Very cold, but not cold enough for motel vouchers or to open extra shelters," she said.

He nodded. "I hope you won't tell anyone about this," Walter said quietly. "We got some cold weather ahead of us and–"

"Not to worry, Walter," she said. "I'm a temp."

"All that means is you don't have to care enough to care, Mabel."

"Yeah, but it also means I don't have to be an asshole. Your secrets are safe with me." She smiled and held out her hand.

They shook on it and when her taxi arrived, Walter watched until they pulled away from the curb. Hackenbush couldn't tell if there were other watchers; it was too dark in the lobby to see them. She thought she could feel them, but she was very tired and might have been mistaken.

She was a few minutes late the next morning, but not because of the night before.

"Driver! Wait! There are people coming!"

Minding her own damn business, Hackenbush was half way out the back doors and looked down Wilshire to where a middle aged Latina and her three little girls were running for the bus. Holding the back door open, she looked the other direction, where a young guy she saw on this bus every morning was banging on the front doors, yelling at the driver to wait. "Hey, bus driver, can you wait 'til I get out before you split?" she yelled, watching the little family rush past her. A few passengers took up pro or con positions, but most of them couldn't have cared less.

"Let's go, lady!" the driver yelled at her, keeping the front doors firmly closed.

"You got some more customers, dad." One foot in the bus and the other on the pavement; she was dearly hoping this driver wasn't going to make an example of her by ripping her in half.

The young guy kept knocking on the front doors while Hackenbush kept the back doors open. It was a stand-off of sorts and the bus driver finally allowed the Latina and her family to get on the bus. Hackenbush had just barely let the back doors swing shut behind her when the driver expressed his displeasure by jerking the bus into traffic and cutting off a Mercedes. Well, that was all right, they were supposed to have great brakes and these didn't even squeal.

"Thank you for helping me."

She glanced over her shoulder at the young guy. He'd run up behind her and was a little out of breath. "Oh, you're welcome."

"I see you on that bus all the time," he said. "I think we work in the same building. I'm on five and you're on three."

"What?"

"I'm on the fifth floor, Oberlin Re, and you're on the third floor, Withers and Sons."

"Oh, yeah," she said, and they fell silent as they crossed Wilshire. One needed to concentrate when crossing Wilshire.

"My name is Alan," he said when they were safely on the other side.

"Mine's Mabel; nicetomeetcha." She waved at the security guys and stepped into the elevator. "Five, is it?" she asked, punching her floor and his.

"Yes. I'd like to thank you for helping back there," he said.

"Got a couple of grand I could have?" she thought wryly, but said, "You did. You're welcome."

"Maybe I could buy you lunch today?" he said, holding the elevator open on Three.

"Today is not looking very good..."

"Tomorrow?"

"Tomorrow is worse."

"Friday?"

"Ummmm..."

"Next week?"

"That would work," she said. "We'll figure it out on the bus, hey?"

"That would be–" the elevator began to ding impatiently at him, so he just said, "Thanks; bye," and was gone.

"Making friends, Hackenbush?" Paula asked, looking pointedly at her wristwatch.

"Yes indeed, Paula, as well as championing the right of any reasonable persons to ride the bus as long as they have the fare in correct change." She left the office manager to ponder this egalitarian (with caveats) idea and went to her desk. There she found a new stack of work and a thank-you note from Charles in his lovely penmanship for the work she did last night. She put her stuff down and dove right in; at least it made the day go by quickly.

About three thirty that afternoon, Suzy rolled Withers Senior into Charles's office, where the big, serious clients, who were keeping Hackenbush so busy, were already waiting. Obviously dismissed from her Withers-pushing duty, Suzy strolled out and asked Hackenbush if she wanted to go get coffee at the Royale.

"I want to, but I need to stick around in case they need something stapled together," she said, clearing off the chair by her desk. "But sit here and keep me company, if you've nothing better to do."

"Not until I am called," Suzy drawled, looking for something to play with on Hackenbush's desk. "Is there coffee here? Can I have some?"

"Sure; I'll even fetch it for you."

And as if on cue, Withers Junior buzzed for coffee for six to be sent in. However, Paula, especially watchful when there were big billable clients in the office, intercepted the order. "I'll get it, Mabel."

"Don't you trust me, Paula?" Hackenbush asked at the coffee maker. She was pouring a cup for Suzy first. "Think I might start yelling 'Long live anarchy' or try to pick up the least fossilized guy in there?"

"Nothing of the kind, Mabel," Paula assured her. "Anna warned me that you're a terrible waitress and not to ask you to do that."

"S'true, I hate getting coffee," she agreed. "It annoys me irrationally." She did hold the door open for the tray-bearing office manager after she gave Suzy her cup.

"Well, we can't have that," Paula said vaguely on her way into Charles's office. "Thanks."

"You're welcome." She went back to Suzy and her desk.

"Thanks; this is terrible coffee," Suzy said.

"You're welcome; it's office coffee, it's not supposed to be good. We might learn to like it here if the coffee was really good." Hackenbush sat down and watched the tall, slender drink of water, better known as Belinda Rafeson, glide into Frank's office.

Paula came out with the coffee tray and leaned against Mabel's desk. She sighed with relief and told the dancer and her fellow vocalist that everybody was still smiling in there.

"Have they had any coffee yet?" Mabel asked.

"Not yet," Paula said, watching Frank and Belinda get into the elevator. "Now, there's an accident waiting to happen."

"What?" Suzy asked. She'd seen none of it because she was wedged into the far corner of Hackenbush's secretarial alcove.

"Frank and Belinda."

"Charles's brother and girlfriend? Old Charles says they're just friends." Suzy stirred her coffee, hoping the oil might spread out a little more. She looked up to find the vocalists mildly (Hackenbush) and very (Paula) interested.

"Oh?" Paula asked. Hackenbush hit the save key on her document.

"I wheeled the old boy into a party last night and the younger generation was there, all three of them," Suzy told her. "More sparks flew between Frank and the chick than between the chick and Young Charles. At least I thought so, but Old Charles says I'm nuts, so I must be."

"Hmmmmm, I..." Paula broke off whatever she was going to say to answer the phone in her office.

"Any thoughts on this, Mabel?" Suzy asked.

"Hard to tell, darlin', I only met them for a minute last night," Hackenbush said, omitting Frank's messy confession she'd tried not to hear over the Dictaphone. "I try not to get too interested in other people's sex lives."

"Since you don't have one."

"Touché, baby."

"Why is that, Mabel? You're not repulsive, why don't you attract some love?" Suzy asked her.

"Dunno, Suzy, I can't even attract Tough Love these days anymore," Mabel said.

"Just say no, Mabel." Suzy shook her finger at her.

"'No, Mabel'. Seriously, Suzy, I can't tell if I have bad taste in men and so have bad luck with them or if it's the bad luck that causes the bad taste. And then I have a Seventies mentality about sex and hate latex. It's enough to make a girl do drugs."

"No, it's not," Suzy said firmly. "What's your Seventies mentality got to do with latex?"

"In the Seventies it was all 'let's go to your place' after five minutes of conversation–"

"Oh yeah. Sometimes we only got as far as the car."

"The good old days," Hackenbush agreed. "Now if you slip up and forget the condom–"

"Or the guy refuses–"

"And it's the wrong guy, you're dead," Hackenbush said.

"It is almost enough to make a girl do drugs." Suzy smiled at her.

"Nah, I have even less self-control on drugs; let me stick to booze, which I can still handle."

"Amen to that." They clinked coffee cups and made faces; this coffee was even worse lukewarm. "I have an interesting story for you, Mabel."

"Oh?"

"About Aline Jones and Withers the Older. You've heard of Aline Jones, haven't you?" Suzy watched

Hackenbush think it over and then shake her head. "That's because you're a savage and a singer. Aline Jones was the hottest dancer in LA and maybe the West Coast thirty or so years ago. Kind of a cross between Josephine Baker and Anna Pavlova."

"Skinny white girl wearing a string of bananas?" Hackenbush asked.

"No. Gorgeous black woman with grace and fire," Suzy said. "And technique to die for. And like me, she was too tall and too curvy to be a big time ballerina and this was before Lula Washington hit the scene and well before there was a serious dance community in LA–"

"Like there is now?"

"Do you want to hear this story?"

"Sure! Tell me what a gorgeous, genius, black better-than-a-ballerina would have to do with Withers Senior Why, not even on drugs would I touch him with a ten foot practice barre."

"Really, Mabel? I imagine thirty-five years ago he looked a lot like Withers Junior." Suzy paused to let that sink in. "Anyway, I spent yesterday at Withers Senior's house in Hancock Park–"

"Oh, I approve of Hancock Park."

"Me, too. It's a nice place, nice garden. Anyway, in his home office there's pictures of him and his wife, who I didn't recognize, and pictures of him and Aline, who I did. He was impressed that I knew who she was and then he told me that she's Frank's mother."

Hackenbush leaned back and held up her hand while she got her question to formulate. "Are you telling me this guy has pictures of his wife and his girlfriend in the same area?"

"Yeah, and here's the kicker: it's a long-standing and venerable tradition in the Withers clan to have a fancy wife and a fancier mistress," Suzy said, lowering her voice. "Frank and Charles Junior are only about five years apart in age. How fast d'you think Charles Senior got set up with Aline after the wedding?"

"If not before the wedding," Hackenbush mused. "And then he gave Frank a job at the firm. Well, that was white of–"

"Mabel, it's Withers and Sons, Frank's a partner," Suzy corrected her. "Withers Senior paid for all of Frank's education, private schools, UCLA, law school, the works."

"And what did Mrs. Withers think?"

"He never said. Must not have been an issue for him."

"UCLA, huh, that's public-spirited of the old boy."

"The old boy went to USC, I saw his diploma, and that's where Charles Junior went," Suzy said. "And Charles Junior went to Loyola Law School and Frank went to Southwestern, so, yeah he paid for his education, but not as much as he paid for Charles."

"Well, it's more than anybody ever did for us, Suzy."

"True enough."

"It does seem like kind of a drag that Frank worked just as hard as anyone on this deal the Charleses are discussing today and he ain't in the finale," Hackenbush said. "It's unfair."

"Whoever told you life was fair, Mabel?" Suzy asked. "And besides, if he was in that meeting he couldn't be sneaking around with Belinda, could he?"

"Well, maybe life is more fair than we realize, Suzy."

"Hmmmmm."

They drank coffee in silence for a while. Hackenbush smoked while Suzy looked on. "How'd'ya like your job so far?" Mabel asked, pinching a shred of tobacco off her tongue.

"Oh fine. I get out law books, make photocopies, read legal stuff to him—his eyes are going, I think—make decent coffee and generally do gofer stuff," she said. "It's not a career for a dancer, but it will do until I figure something else out."

"Like what?"

"I don't know. Open a dance school, throw myself off a bridge, give a solo recital, something."

"I vote for one and three, Suzy," Hackenbush said, listening to the voices in the hall. "Look sharp, hon."

They had the professional secretary look going when Charles brought out a stack of paper for Hackenbush to photocopy. When she got back to her desk from that errand, she saw Paula going into his office with her Notary stamp.

"There, Suzy, you could become a Notary Public," Hackenbush said, settling back into her chair. "Like Paula."

"Or throw myself off a bridge. I'd rather be a vocalist like Paula before that."

"She really had it, didn't she?"

"Or you, Hackenbush, you really have it, too."

"And I'm still using it."

They rapped their knuckles on the desk. Not long afterwards, the meeting broke up and Suzy vanished with Withers Senior. Frank rolled back in, without Belinda, and shut himself up in his office until six. Charles and Hackenbush stayed in the office until eight-thirty, working separately on the deal he'd just closed.

"Thanks for working long hours, Mabel," he said in the elevator.

"Oh, you're welcome," she said, getting out at the lobby. He took the elevator down to the parking garage.

In the shadowy lobby, Hackenbush looked around for Walter. The guard on duty told her Walter didn't come in until ten. She asked him to say "hi" for her and, clutching her taxi voucher, went out to get into her luxurious taxi. She thought she recognized a few shadows around the park, but it was really too dark to tell.

The next morning Bobby brought his guitar to the office and told his mother he had a lesson right after work. This was true, and what was also true was that Carlos and Shorty were meeting him in the parking garage at twelve sharp. They would then join Hackenbush on the roof for a quick rehearsal of *The Goodbye Look* and a discussion of the upcoming gig.

Bobby was in heaven. He'd gone to Tower Records on Sunset to get the LP and had played that song at least a dozen times last night. He could now play it from memory and knew all the words. He was ready; he was possibly over-prepared, but he was ready.

Just before noon, he saluted Hackenbush on his way down to get Shorty and Carlos.

She smiled, slipped on her dancing shoes and raced up the stairs. Stepping onto the roof, Hackenbush squinted against the winter sun and consequently failed to see that Charles Withers was there with her. She walked to the ledge and did a few stretches while she waited for the guys to show up.

Withers was annoyed and amused to see Hackenbush on his roof. He came up there to think, or fume or sometimes laugh or just to get some privacy. Today he was there to think about the new deal he was working on, and his father's new assistant.

He'd interrogated Paula about Suzanne Reed and decided he'd allow Suzy to live. After all, his father hadn't turned up at all today and that was a blessing for everyone. Charles wondered how much Hackenbush had to do with bringing Suzy on board, so he was pleased to see her on the roof since he wanted to talk to her anyway. However, she seemed wrapped up in her own thoughts, so Charles didn't disturb her. He was content to spy on her from behind the stairs landing, which was the only structure one could lurk behind on this particular roof.

Charles did a quick step around the back of the landing when he heard steps. Hackenbush said something he didn't catch and then she and the newcomers moved to the center of the roof and made shuffling, clunking noises. Slipping around the structure, Charles found himself with a good view of Hackenbush, Bobby and two seedy-looking guys; a short dark one and a pale lean one about Hackenbush's height, who had an unhealthy pallor. Or maybe he was an inch or two taller as Hackenbush was wearing a flashy pair of high heels. Charles thought these were rather sexy shoes, unlike anything he'd seen on her feet since she'd arrived. Anyway. The dark one was sitting cross-legged and had a pair of bongos between his knees. He was talking to Bobby, who holding a guitar and listening very intently. They nodded at each other and the dark guy clucked his tongue and shrugged his shoulders a few times and they started to play a Latin, or something like that, sounding tune.

Hackenbush and the pale guy danced a few steps, rather remarkably well, Withers thought. Her dancing was quite charming and watching her took up all his attention.

And then she sang.

He was so engrossed, he nearly jumped out of his skin when Paula appeared in his peripheral vision.

"So, this is what's up up here," she growled.

Charles could only nod and wonder how she could speak while Hackenbush was singing. He did notice that Paula had an analytical, if not critical, look on her face.

"She's not bad, is she?" Paula asked absently when Hackenbush had finished the verse and was dancing with Shorty.

"Ummmm." Charles managed to grunt before Mabel started singing again.

And then the song was over and Bobby said, "I think the word in that line is, 'skinny,' not 'stringy.'" Charles saw Paula wince and noticed the two guys wince as well. "What's that about?" he whispered to Paula.

"Never tell a singer she's got the words wrong," Paula whispered back, keeping an eye on her son. "Words are what singers are all about."

Paula coiled to spring when Hackenbush swiveled on her heels to face Bobby.

"I find the word 'stringy' so much more evocative than 'skinny', don't you, Bobby?" the singer drawled in a dangerously sonorous and bell-like voice. Possibly it was her outdoor voice or her don't-fuck-with-me voice. Paula didn't know her well enough to know which. She was prepared to lunge for her throat if Hackenbush got any rougher with her child.

Behind Hackenbush, the pale guy was making frantic 'just agree with her' signs to Bobby, who sensibly did just that.

"Oh, of course, Dr. Hackenbush! I was just so knocked sideways by it, I don't know what I was thinking!" he said, a little louder than necessary.

"You learn fast, my little one," Paula thought, relaxing again.

Hackenbush smiled and said something Paula and Charles didn't catch and the song started again. There was some discussion and a few alterations in the dance steps and two more repetitions before Hackenbush looked at her watch and cursed.

Paula looked her watch—lunch break was over—and suggested that she and Withers go back to the office before the band caught them. They took the stairs quickly and silently. In the office, Paula followed Withers into his lair.

"Is that okay with you, Mr. Withers?" she asked. "The rehearsal up there?" she added when he seemed dazed.

"I suppose," he said, thinking of insurance issues now that he was back in lawyer mode. "If it's not a regular occurrence. Why are they up there anyway?"

Paula said she didn't know, but promised she'd try to find out. She went downstairs to grab a sandwich from the snack bar. On her way back up, she saw the dark guy and the pale guy driving off in an old, battered sedan. In the office, she found Hackenbush at her desk, typing away from the Dictaphone as if she'd been there all day. However, there was a stack of postcards on the edge of her desk for a Saturday gig at the Island Room that hadn't been there before and Paula found a couple of these on her own desk. One had a note, 'would LOVE to see YOU there', scribbled on it. She kept that one and gave the other to Charles, who stopped everything he was doing and put it in his briefcase.

"Hackenbush, I'm sorry to ask again, can you work late tonight?"

Hackenbush looked up at Charles and had the tiniest moment of hesitation before she said yes. Usually Paula, not Charles, asked her to stay late and there was something new and odd in his voice, especially in the way he thanked her. Not alarming or annoying, just a little too enthusiastic for the subject. It sent her guard up, the same way her guard went up when a guy got too friendly between sets, when all Hackenbush wanted to do was drink her drink in peace for a few minutes. But, oh well, time and a half was time and a half.

Having overheard Withers asking Hackenbush to stay late and recalling his interest in the singer on the roof that afternoon, Paula's guard was up too. Especially since she knew there wasn't enough work to keep Hackenbush, or any of them, overtime.

Even Bobby gave Hackenbush a funny look when she told him she was staying late. "Why?"

Hackenbush thought the question rather husbandly, but answered it anyway. "Mr. Withers asked me to."

"Which one?"

"Withers Junior"

"Oh," he said. He said good night to Adela and then to the redheaded guy as they went by. The office was really clearing out that night. "You'll be the only one here with him."

"So?" She watched him fidget. "Men are so cute when they fidget," she thought.

"So...so, nothing." He shrugged and said good night.

About an hour later, Paula came by in her coat to tell Hackenbush she was leaving and give her a taxi voucher. She said good night and then fidgeted, which annoyed Hackenbush, who thought women should never fidget; it was so unbecoming. "Um, Mabel, did you ever know a club owner named Joe York?"

"I think he was before my time, Paula," Hackenbush said, offering her a cigarette and lighting it for her.

Paula took a lung-full of smoke and exhaled. "Yeah, well, this guy had a fold-out bed in his office."

"What club owner in the history of the species didn't have a fold-out bed in his office?" Mabel asked, wondering what the hell...

"Withers Junior has one in his office," Paula whispered.

"A club owner?"

"No, a fold-out bed and he asked me to leave just now," Paula hissed at her. "So, I am leaving, but I'm just telling you...telling you about Joe York. Dig?"

"To China," Hackenbush rapped out. "I'll keep an eye out for Joe York. Withers Junior, I think I can handle on my own."

"He's done this before," Paula said softly.

"Joe York?"

"No, Withers Junior, he's put the moves on secretaries—"

"Just the moves or is there violence?"

"No! Of course not!"

"I'm just asking, Paula. I guess I don't have to borrow your pepper spray then? Ha ha."

"Ha ha, Mabel. Don't say I didn't warn you. Good night and good luck," Paula said, stubbing out her cigarette.

"Thanks, sister, see you tomorrow," she said to her back. "Think positive thoughts, okay?" She could almost feel the office manager roll her eyes.

Hackenbush merely lowered her own eyes and looked around her desk for some work. There wasn't any so she made some. She balanced her checkbook, triaged all the little pieces of paper crammed in her purse, updated her 'to do' list, and had a good start on a letter to her council person about the tragedy known as life in Lincoln Heights since the library closed. It would be better read aloud and she put some serious thought into making an appointment to perform it. Or better yet, set to music, it could be... Of course the phone would buzz just when absurdist inspiration hit and it was Charles, asking her to step into his office.

Which she did and found his desk as denuded of work as hers, only his desk had a bottle and a pair of thick crystal Old-Fashioned glasses. "At least we're not shooting tequila tonight," she thought, but said, and sweetly, too, "You rang."

"Yes, Hackenbush, I wanted to thank you for all your hard work this week," he said.

"Oh, you're welcome," she said and watched him fidget, thinking: "Men are so cute when they fidg–"

"Drink?"

"Sure," she said, taking a client chair across the desk from him. "What are we drinking?"

"Scotch all right with you?" He tilted a voluptuous and unopened bottle toward her and she caught a glimpse of the word 'Macallan'.

Now, any lady who spends as much time in saloons as Hackenbush did knows her booze. She knew that this was the Scotch saloonkeepers keep locked in their offices and only bring out for high rollers. Thus far in her career, Hackenbush had only progressed as far up the Scotch food chain as

Longmorn and that was at a wake, so she wasn't sure it counted as a real Scotch experience. Therefore she was impressed that Charles would be so kind as to come on to her with such fancy whisky. Or perhaps he just wanted to be sure to get her drunk without her realizing it. Well, he picked the wrong vocalist to try that on. But all Hackenbush said just then was, "Oh, what a pretty bottle," and accepted the three fingers he poured out. They clinked glasses to toast the deal Withers and Sons had just closed and sat back to savor the liquor.

One of the many things Hackenbush could do well was drink. And this booze was so good, she didn't even want a cigarette with it; it was fine all by itself in her mouth. Of course the glow started behind her sternum and then migrated to her solar plexus, staked its claim and rolled back up like smoke and filled her shoulders. She finished the first glass in her usual time and noticed Charles bolting at least half of his to keep up with her. "Well, there's your first mistake, Casanova," she thought.

"Isn't this good?" she drawled, accepting another glass.

"Yes, very," he said, sipping along with her. "Paula tells me you're a very famous vocalist in town."

"Paula told you that?"

"Well, actually it was Bobby."

"Ah. Well, I do all right as a vocalist; some people seem to like it."

"Can you make a living at that?" he asked.

"Oh, fairly well, my needs are few," she said, pushing her empty glass within pouring range. He downed what was left in his before setting them both up again.

"But here you are working as a temp..." He trailed off meaningfully, momentarily lulled by Hackenbush's polite attention.

This was a male mannerism that drove Hackenbush nuts because she thought everyone should finish his sentences and if he has a question, ask the fucker, don't make her guess. So she merely smiled encouragingly, as if to give him time to finish whatever he was trying to say. Smart guy; he figured it out in less than ten seconds.

"I mean, here you are temping for extra money, I suppose, since you probably have enough singing work," he said. "Why is that?"

"Which, Mr. Withers? Why am I temping or why don't I have enough singing work or why am I here?"

"All of those," he said, recovering a little.

"Well, I've made a few sacrifices for music, but I do like to stay above the poverty line," she said, polishing off her drink. "I don't mind typing for a few weeks to get the savings revved-up a little for a rainy day." No point telling him it was monsoon season and these future revved-up savings were already in first gear and heading for a new Ghia transmission and new baritone uke. "Of course, in a perfect world, we'd all make enough money at what we love and have health insurance, too."

"Well, you could have health insurance if you got a regular job," he said, pouring for both of them.

"I and everybody like me could have health insurance if it was a priority for our government," she said, tipping the glass back.

"Why should our government look after what you neglect?"

"Because a fifteen-minute test of the useless Star Wars missile defense costs three billion dollars and that's a lot of healthcare in anybody's book." She watched him over her glass. "And besides, do we really need space age warfare to kick the shit out of a little island like Grenada? I mean, they could have sent in the Marine Corps Marching Band and gotten about the same result."

"Grenada aside, I'm not sure I like my tax dollars going for missile defense either," he admitted. "I dislike paying taxes in general."

"Really? Why? You get such great stuff for the money most of the time."

"Like what?"

She tossed back her drink; he tossed back his drink and poured again. "Like the courts," she said. "As an attorney you must get some mileage out of those."

"Mainly they annoy me."

"The laws or the architecture?"

"Oh, neither, only the rulings against me bother me quite a bit." He leaned forward and eyed her over his desk. "What other great stuff am I getting for my tax dollars?"

"Federal or local?"

"Federal."

"National Endowment for the Arts."

"Never use it."

"Ever go to the Phil or LACMA?"

"Of course."

"You think they run on entrance fees and overpriced sodas alone?"

"Never thought about it," he said, carefully enunciating. "You sound like you like paying taxes."

"No more than you, probably, and proportionally, I pay more than you because you have more money than I do," she said, holding out her glass for more and watching him hastily finish his pour them both another. "A couple of grand is walking-around money for a guy like you. For me, it's a major investment."

"There's nothing wrong with having money."

"Nor is there with paying for truth, justice, education, healthcare, art, infrastructure, and the American way," she said, and all that make her throat dry. She took a sip and rolled the whisky around in her mouth. "No, nothing wrong with that. Besides, my taxes only pay for certain things."

"Howzat?"

"I write on my check, in the memo section, where I want the money applied," she said. "Don't you?" He shook his head and then looked dizzy. "Usually I write NEA, but last year I saw an article about how impoverished the Customs Department is so I put them down. I don't know that my fifteen hundred will keep them going very long, but it's the thought that counts." She watched his eyes cross. "This year I'm torn between yellow legal pads for Federal Judges and slide rules for mechanical engineers at NASA," she said leaning her elbows on Charles's desk and looking deeply into his eyes. It was a soulful moment, watching lust war with confusion warring with the Republican fiscal policy locked in combat with, well, more lust. A liberal would have made his move by now, or at least realized Hackenbush had drunk him under the table. But not this guy; he still thought he had his finger on the pulse of the situation when he actually wasn't even near the bangle bracelet of the situation. So, in this soulful moment, Hackenbush looked into the bottom of Charles Withers Junior's soul; it didn't take very long as there wasn't much of it showing around the greed, intolerance, arrogance and, well, lust, again, but oh well, there's more truth in liquor than we know. And brushing all the things Charles was not and never would be aside, Hackenbush asked what was really on her mind, "Can I have little more of that?" she asked, tilting her chin at the Macallan.

He poured; they drank in silence.

"Well, I must be going," she said, polishing off her drink.

"Must you?"

"Yes, it's eleven-thirty and I have to work tomorrow." Standing up made her realize that she was drunker than she thought, but still less smashed than Charles. To compensate for this, she simply moved and spoke more slowly than usual. Nicotine would help; at least, that was her story and she was sticking to it. "Amazing how fast time flies when you're drinking," she said going to her desk and successfully getting a cigarette out and lit. She heard Charles moving around in his office, more like stumbling around in his office, and decided it was time for her to go home. She packed up and called a taxi.

Just to have something to say, she repeated, "Well, I must be going," as Charles staggered up to her desk.

"Oh? Must you? I'll give you a lift home."

"Oh, thanks, but I'm sure that's out of your way," she said, heading for the elevator. "And I've already called a taxi."

Charles could move fast when he was so inclined and had his briefcase and coat when he got into the elevator with her. "I'm sure I could give you a lift," he told her, standing a little too close.

"I'm not sure you should be driving anybody anywhere,"

Hackenbush told him.

"Oh really? I've only had as much to drink as you," he said, getting even closer.

"Which was a lot and, please notice, I'm taking a cab home, compliments of the firm," she said, waving her taxi voucher at him.

Luckily, the elevator slogged to the first floor and opened in the lobby. Hackenbush cheerfully greeted Walter by name and introduced him to Charles. "Who should not be driving, but plans to anyway," she added, peering out the front doors, trying to make her taxi materialize out of sheer will.

"Perhaps I could get you a taxi, too, Mr. Withers," Walter suggested after getting a whiff and look at both of them. "Possibly you could share Miss Hackenbush's taxi."

"Oh! Walter, no! Impossible!" Miss Hackenbush practically shouted in alarm. "This guy can't possibly live anywhere near Lincoln Heights."

"Why not?" they asked.

"It's very exclusive; kind of place you have to earn the right to live in."

"How so?" Charles asked, sobering a little in the cool, under-heated, un-insulated lobby.

"By never making assumptions about anyone, never flaunting what one has to those who don't have it, and never leaving your car out of gear when you're parked on Thomas Street," Hackenbush said vaguely.

There was some silence while Charles and Walter stared at her, trying to figure out if she'd just said something so profound they couldn't understand it or so cryptic they couldn't understand it or so stupid no one sane, sober or not, could understand it. Then they looked at each other and shrugged. 'It's a mystery,' their shoulders seemed to say.

In the midst of these meditations, a yellow sedan pulled up in front and flashed its lights. "My chariot awaits!" Hackenbush cried and flung herself out the door and into it before either man could react.

It was a relief when she was gone. Somehow the lobby seemed bigger, it was definitely calmer and certainly less hip than it had been a minute ago.

Charles looked away from the street and back at Walter, who seemed to be mulling over a question he wanted to ask. Well, the poor guard had asked it before and Charles decided to spare them both the embarrassment of having Walter offer to get him a taxi again, so he said, "I think I'll go up and take a nap in my office before I got home."

Walter simply said, "Yes, sir." He watched the elevator lights go up to the third floor and not down to the parking garage with some relief. He truly hated to see people waste themselves in any way shape or form, truly he did.

The next morning she ran into Alan on the bus. He was glad to see her; she could tell even though she was slightly hung-over. "Where you been, Alan?"

"Trying to avoid that driver we had on Wednesday. You?"

"The bus comes, I get on it and so far nobody's shot at me," she said. "I certainly hope that driver has better things to do than remember passengers that annoyed him. He'd have no time for anything else if he did."

"People stay mad about the damnedest things sometimes," Alan said, watching the rain roll down the windows. And then he won Hackenbush's heart forever by giving his seat to an old guy.

Because there were no bus rider rebellions that morning, Hackenbush was on time. But what she walked into was not the intense, but orderly business premises she'd grown used to; no, this was a tense and angry place and most of the staff seemed to be either in Charles's office, staring at him and his fold-out bed, which was folded out. She sidled up behind Paula and said, "Hey, that does fold out, don't it?"

Paula wheeled around and snarled, "Where the hell have you been?"

"On the bus, voyaging to my fabulous temp job."

"You weren't here all night?"

"No," Hackenbush said, beginning to catch on. "And I've got a taxi receipt to prove it."

"I hardly need that," Paula said, still pissed off. "Excuse me, Mr. Withers, I seem to have misread the situation. All right, everyone, let's get to work." She herded the firm's employees out into the hall.

Hackenbush went to her desk, changed her soggy shoes and went back to Charles's office. Not into the office, she just leaned on the door jamb, one foot in the hall, one inside. He'd folded the bed up and was tying his tie. This fascinated Hackenbush because most of the men she knew seldom wore ties, and when they did, she never got to seem them tie them. It looked like a very complex accomplishment and she was impressed. But she didn't let it show and simply asked him how his head was.

"Oh, fine," he said, adjusting the knot. "I've never had a bad hangover from that scotch. You?"

"Me? I'm okay," she said, thinking she had enjoyed drinking with this guy, even though he was totally wrong for her, and taken to boot. "I'm glad you didn't drive home, even though you weren't too thrashed. All that fresh air would have wrecked the high. Like it did for me. That's why I tried to get in the cab before I got too much oxygen."

"Ah."

"Your staff seems to think I was here all last night."

"And several of them wanted to lynch me for it, at least Bobby did. Your timely appearance saved the day."

"Glad to hear it." She waved at Bobby watching from the mailroom and turned back to Charles. "Don't be too hard on Bobby. The poor kid got raised right and thinks every lady needs a knight in shining armor. He'll get over that someday."

"Doesn't every lady need a knight?"

"Nah; most of us just need a helping hand now and then."

"Hmmm," he said. And since he had no further comment on the subject, he picked up a pair of mini cassettes and handed them to her. She took the hint—obviously the work day had well and truly begun—and went off to type like a madwoman for eight hours.

And it was only eight hours that day. Everybody except Paula, who often worked late, cleared out at five.

Hackenbush slept late on Sa'day—sorry, Saturday—and, except for a quick trip to the grocery store ostensibly for perishables, but mainly for cigarettes, and a dash to her bank, was in the house all day. Not that that bothered her; she had plenty of reading, music arranging, singing and general and unfocused lying around to do. Because what little money there was in her checkbook was already balanced, which was one chore done on the 'to do,' she cleaned the kitchen and ticked off another chore. Feeling good about this, she felt better when the mailman left her Mr. Tanaka's check and the Temp Insanity one for those first two days at Withers and Sons, which was damn good and generous since she only got there at noon a week ago Thursday. "So long ago; lawdy, time flies when you're working days," she thought, endorsing her checks on her way out the door. With a little exertion she was able to sprint down to her bank and deposit them before the one o'clock closing. Walking back home, she treated herself to a half a chicken at Chapalita. Not that all of her money problems were solved, but at least there was a little more of the stuff sloshing around in her account.

Around six, Shorty turned up with his suitcase and some chow mein from the New Won Kok restaurant. He'd called earlier to tell her his house sitting job was done and ask if he could sleep there at least that night. Hackenbush never minded sharing her bed with Shorty; he was a harmless guy and a peaceful sleeper. And in winter she could leave the heat off a little longer as long as she could curl up with him in the morning.

Luis showed up around eight to give them a lift to the gig. They arrived early to the mostly deserted Island Room. The dinner rush was over and the music rush wouldn't start until about ten. The owner, a kindly Filipino guy named Juan, fed them lavishly. Dinner was usually part of gigs like this, however, Hackenbush had had her share of gigs where dinner was a bowl of soup and crackers. But Juan was a right thinking kind of guy and gave them roast beef with a sweet teriyaki sauce, baked yams, their insides scooped out and whipped with butter and honey and put back in, zucchini and mushrooms stir fried with garlic and tossed with a little vinegar and chunky sea salt. Hackenbush was in heaven and thought she could fall in love with this guy had his wife not beaten her to it. For dessert they got the Island Room's famous ice cream with fruit and sprinkled with grated coconut. "Man, daddy, I'll sing here anytime you got a night for me," she sighed at Juan.

"Carlos says the secret to great singing from you is to feed you right, diva baby," Juan said, pouring her a coffee.

"That's true; she eats her weight in sushi every week at the Lotus room."

"WANG!" she cried and leapt up to hug him.

The skinny Chinese bartender took a seat next to her and ordered a salad and coffee for himself. "I miss you and the Lotus Room," he said.

"How are you, the Lotus Room and, most of all, how's Mr. Tanaka?" she asked, refusing a cigarette because she wanted to keep tasting her dinner for a while longer. "I hear he might start loving me again, as soon as the insurance company check clears."

"He might love you a lot when the club re-opens next month," Wang said. "I called in to find out what hellhole I was bartending in and his secretary said they were getting about three calls a day from people who want to know either where you are or when you'll be back at the Lotus Room."

Hackenbush exchanged puzzled looks with Shorty.

"Don't ask me, Mabel, I only call in every other day and disguise my voice," he said.

"Huh, crazy," she said. "Nice to be loved and missed."

"Yeah, girl, it's gonna be jammed here tonight," Wang said. "The word is out this might be your last gig for a while. That's why I came early; good food and a quiet word with you."

"I'm fifty percent honored and a hundred percent touched." She smiled at him; he was truly her favorite bartender in town: wise, compassionate and generous with the gin. "I hope we'll all be together again soon, Wang, I miss you, too."

"Cheer up, baby, it's all going your way." Wang was ever the optimist for other people. He was more mysterious about his own hopes and dreams.

"You're never wrong, Wang, so I'll just leave it at that," she said, applying a thick coat of lipstick. They sat in silence, watching the band set up.

Hackenbush was very pleased to see that Joey Bell was their guitar player. He'd been around town forever and was a great accompanist for singers—be they good or be they bad singers—because he gave them a nice, warm and cozy glow to sing in. She'd worked with him once or twice on casuals and would have had him in her band in a second, except he'd never take orders from a chick. He'd made this clear, and there was only one leader in Dr. Hackenbush's Orchestra, so that was out. But he greeted her with a wink and a wave, which was as close to a bow and kiss on the hand a guy like that got.

The kit drummer was a new guy in town whose name escaped Hackenbush at the moment. She did notice he was tall, dark and languid, which could be trouble if he expected the bass player to keep time while he grooved on cosmic subjects. On the other hand, his drums were very basic— snare, tom-toms, bass, cymbals—no toys or chimes or other exotic materials in sight. This could mean he got a lot out of simple stuff, something Hackenbush could admire since she did that herself, or he was just a skins metronome and she, Luis and Joey had a long night ahead of them. Carlos was Carlos; he'd play whatever felt right and, miraculously, it would be right.

The band would play most of the first set by themselves while the room filled up. A steady stream of people came up to greet Hackenbush with a hug, a kiss, or a manly handshake. Those who knew her didn't linger and those who didn't left pretty quickly when they saw the abstracted look in her eyes she always had before the first song.

Before the first song was her hell time. All her doubts and fears welled up and taunted her. It was a basic form of stage fright—some actors welcomed it, some dancers reveled in it—Hackenbush surrendered to it with much bad grace, but all performers knew it and knew it well.

That pre-first-song twist in her gut had gone away once,

long ago, when her heart froze over the remains of a love affair gone wrong. She went numb; couldn't sing, couldn't think, couldn't do more than survive. And then, gradually, she came back to life and welcomed her pre-first-song nerves back, practically threw a party for them. Eventually, that wore off too, so that now they just annoyed her because she could sing again and the joyful shout in her voice might be tinged with more sadness than before, but who cared when she was soaring?

So she said hi to Cody and Ross when they came to sit with her. They took seats behind her, Ross on her left, Cody on her right, which was where they were when they were all on stage. "Whaddya think of this drummer, Ross?" she asked, leaning back.

"Hmmm, pretty spare stuff, but right where he needs to be all the time," Ross said. "Seems like he'll stay outta your way, but don't expect a rescue if you get the time snarled up."

"I got Luis to rescue me for that, dad," she said.

"And Joey to jump in if you get really lost," Cody said, laying a long dark hand on her shoulder.

"What the hell are you two worried about?" she asked, turning around.

"*I Won't Dance* cha cha cha!" Ross chanted at her, "by that famous salsa composer Herome Kern."

"Ai ai ai, señorita!" Cody taunted softly.

"Yeah, well, hopefully I won't have to shoot my way out of that song," she said, listening to Carlos solo himself into a corner.

"It's not you I'm worried about, Mabel," Cody said, watching Luis set the band back on track. Carlos could catch up, or not, whenever or however he did. They listened in silence, trying to get a feel for where the evening was going, musically, that is.

Hackenbush's current guitar player joined them, he took a seat on her right.

"Hey," she said, glancing over at him.

"Hey," Gregg said, his eyes fixed Joey Bell. "I had a couple of lessons with that guy." He jerked his chin at the stage. "He said I stank."

"Did you?" Hackenbush asked.

"Dunno," Gregg said. "You hired me about then, so I must not stink." He offered Hackenbush a cigarette, which she refused, and lit one for himself. "So I dunno why he said that."

"He might have been protecting his market," Ross said.

"How so?" Gregg asked.

"If he told you you stink and you believed him, you might get a job in retail or telemarketing or OD on something," Ross said matter of factly. "And there's one less guitar player in LA."

Hackenbush rolled her eyes at this fiendishly clever and totally goofy idea, but didn't say anything.

"Y'think?" Gregg asked, furrowing his brow in thought.

Hackenbush couldn't take it anymore. "I think Joey is a rotten teacher," she said. "You notice he doesn't have any students."

"Well, neither do I," Gregg said.

"There! Proof positive that you're both great guitar players," she said, hoping to close the subject.

Gregg was silent for a moment. "You think I'm great, Mabel?"

"Dear God, please, take me now," she thought, but it was Carlos, not God, who rescued her.

"Ladies and Gentlemen, we are very pleased to present tonight in the Island Room, direct from the middle class, the fabulous Dr. Hackenbush!"

Hackenbush looked totally calm, but her heart was hammering in her chest like a jackhammer. She strolled onto the little platform and adjusted the mike stand in front of her. She nodded to Joey, who was the de facto leader that night as Carlos was already having some kind of mystical conga experience, and away they went. An eight bar introduction to *Lady Be Good* brought them together as a band, a family, a tribe, a pack, however temporary. And in those last few beats before the first tone came out of her mouth, what was Hackenbush became Hackenbush and the band, her fear shut down and the music had her in its arms.

Charles and Frank found Bobby skulking outside the Island Room.

"What's the matter, Bobby?" Frank asked.

"They won't let me in," he said.

"Why not?" Charles asked.

"I'm not twenty-one."

"Let's see if Uncle Andy can get you in," Charles said, taking a twenty out of his money clip.

It took twin Uncle Andys, but they got Bobby inside and seated with the Withers brothers.

Hackenbush in a dim club had the same effect on Charles as she'd had on the roof; he was mesmerized. Well, so was Bobby; Frank was the only one unfazed at their table.

Frank thought she sang very nicely and looked lovely up there except for the contortions her mouth was doing. When she was silent, listening to the other players, she was almost beautiful, if not luminous.

For Charles it was more elemental; Hackenbush was pure light piercing him with her voice. She was a force that ripped through mundane reality and shimmered with a power he could not understand, but was drawn to anyway. Colors were brighter, sounds were clearer and everything was glowing as if it all might fall away and an entirely new vision appear before him. He ordered a scotch rocks in hopes of taking the edge off it all.

Paula eased in unseen while Hackenbush and Shorty were dancing to *Lady Be Good*. She lurked in the back of the room, staying out of Hackenbush's sight. In her dark glasses, Paula was fairly inconspicuous; several hipsters in the crowd were wearing dark glasses. This meant, however, that Paula couldn't see very well, but she sure could hear, and hear Hackenbush she did sixteen bars later. "Man, is she good, Goddamn, is she good," Paula sighed in her mind, fighting the tide of music that would have carried her away if she'd only let it.

"Is that you behind those Foster Grants, Paula?"

She turned and lifted her shades. "Actually, they're Raybans," she drawled at the guy and then hugged him.

"How've you been, Lowell? Still playing around town?"

"Yeah, solo gigs mostly, some piano bar when I'm desperate, sometimes with a singer," he said, squinting his gray eyes at her. "Are you singing again, yet, Paula?"

"Nah, just raising my kid and working my day gig, that's all," she said and quickly changed the subject. "What do you think of Hackenbush?"

"I think she might be a good singer if she'd cut the comedy and gymnastics," he said, watching Hackenbush dancing with Shorty. "If she got serious, she might someday be as good as you were." He watched Paula wince and continued, "However, I'm going to ask her to sing for me at the Oak Room next week because I can get her for a change. And since you're not around, I guess she'll have to do."

"Lowell," Paula said sharply, taking off her shades. "Listen to her! She's got a beautiful tone, great intonation, phrasing, well, I wouldn't do it that way, but it sure works. You'd be lucky if you could get her!" She lowered her voice when someone shushed her. "Look at her, Lowell, she's all lit up." Paula's eyes filled with tears watching Hackenbush's joy and remember her own, how it felt to let the song course through her body, how it felt to be part of something larger than herself and the band and her life for a few minutes, to rise above her tiny life, spread her wings and soar. And soar, like Hackenbush was now as she wound up for the climax of *Stardust*, which was one of Hackenbush's signature tunes.

Paula thought she did a great job with that song, just the right mix of hope and resignation. The Latin rendition did nothing for her, but one can't have everything. She was mulling this over when she heard an amplified deep male voice say, "Is that you, Paula?" She looked up to find Joey Bell at the mike and looking right at her. He was also holding Hackenbush by the arm, as if to restrain her. Paula generated a weak smile and waved with more gallantry than she felt. She noticed Lowell was standing quite near Joey.

Joey liked Hackenbush, but he liked Paula better. Just then, he was annoyed with Hackenbush, whose tempos, or lack of them, were pissing him off, and he thought she might need a lesson. Lowell's timely arrival with the news that

Paula Dreisler was actually in the room seemed like just the thing to punish Hackenbush with. He leaned over to Carlos and asked him if he minded Paula singing. Carlos had heard of Paula long ago and had no objection.

"You're going to let another singer up here?" Hackenbush hissed angrily under Luis' bass solo. "On my gig?"

"On whose gig, diva baby?" Carlos asked.

Hackenbush hissed a breath out and might have said something regrettable, but Joey hauled her away from Carlos and made her finish the song, which she did with a vengeance. Yeah, she could sing, no doubt about that, but she needed to calm the fuck down. So when the song ended, Joey separated Hackenbush from the microphone and asked, "Is that you, Paula?" He'd watched her wave and smile. "Ladies and Gentlemen, we have another wonderful singer in the audience tonight," he said suavely, tightening his grip on Hackenbush. "Someone LA hasn't heard in far too long and if we're lucky, very lucky, we might be able to persuade her to sing for us tonight. Ladies and Gentlemen, please welcome Miss Paula Dreisler." He let go of the enraged Hackenbush so he could lead the applause. "C'mon up here, Paula!"

Paula advanced through the crowd warily. Joey and Luis looked glad to see her. Carlos and the drummer were curious, but didn't know her and were reserving judgment. Hackenbush looked like she might kill her, or at least maim her, the moment she stepped on the platform. Nothing like that happened, though; Hackenbush simply bared her teeth in what could be mistaken for a smile and stalked over to stand next to Shorty. Paula looked over the crowd, but the lights and smoke and her own nerves made it indistinct. "What?" she asked Joey, who'd spoken to her.

"How about *Night and Day*? You still sing it in G?"

"Yeah, let's do *Night and Day*," Paula said, grateful he'd chosen her talisman song, song she could sing in a coma, and a good song to boot. A strange calm took her as she snapped her fingers, counting off the time and the rush hit her on the first note of the introduction. She stepped off the cliff and soared.

"Shit," Hackenbush thought. "The woman's a genius; possibly a saint. On my gig. And I have to follow that? There is no God. Or She's on vacation."

Shorty leaned close and asked, "Who's the skinny white cat?" He jerked his chin at Lowell.

"Lowell Lowell."

"I heard you the first time," Shorty said.

"That's his name, Lowell Lowell," Hackenbush said, watching Paula. "He's one of those classy piano playing types." She turned her head and found Shorty studying her a little too closely. "Dance. With. Me." She rapped out between her clenched teeth.

And dance they did. Musicians might have hated dancing, or anything else, going on while they were playing, but Shorty and Hackenbush were so amusing to watch and so were tolerated, if not enjoyed. Joey took the first solo, making variation on Paula's lovely phrasing, bringing out the flowing line in his own way. Luis' solo was more disconnected, but still built upon what had gone before. Carlos and the drummer stayed a discreet distance from the fray, still laying down a solid foundation for everyone. Including Hackenbush and Shorty, who were reinventing the rumba for future generations.

They finished their dance as Paula launched into the B section for her finale. Her tone was a little rough from disuse, but she still had the glow about her and her phrasing was as good as ever. She rallied for the ending and her voice came through for her; strong, smoky and warm, she held the last note, suspended it from a gossamer thread, and blew it out like a flame.

There was silence and then there was a lot of applause. Hackenbush found herself yelling "Brava!" over and over. Everybody was on their feet, yelling and stamping; some of them, like Hackenbush, were wiping away those misty tears this kind of performance brings on in certain temperaments, but all of them knew they'd seen something incredible. Only the furniture was unmoved.

Hackenbush pulled herself together and wondered why

she couldn't get audiences to do this when she sang that song. "My version is just as good, really, and–" Luckily her musing was interrupted. "What?" she asked Lowell, standing next to her.

"I said, can you sing for me next week?" he repeated, still applauding for Paula.

"Why don't you ask Paula?" she asked, seeing how focused he was on the office manager.

"She already said no," he said. "Howaboutit?"

"Well, in that case, I'm your girl," she said, handing him a card, and telling him to call her tomorrow—in the afternoon—about the way of the how of it. Oh, and the money of it. She looked up at the band; Paula was shaking hands with the guys. Since Paula appeared to be done singing, Joey must have decided it was a good idea to let Hackenbush sing some more. Hackenbush thought that was right nice of him. She made a faux surprised 'Me?' gesture, pointing to herself, when he beckoned her to the stand. "Excuse me, Lowell, while I go back to work." She and Paula exchanged frostily polite smiles as they passed.

The band launched into *I Won't Dance* and Hackenbush thought it went very well. She saw Charles in the audience, looking lovely and enchanted, and decided the song was going very, very well. At least, she felt good about it even though Joey was scowling at her. "Oh well, can't please everyone," she thought as she danced off with Shorty and left the band to fend for itself.

Lowell found Paula outside taking a break from the intensity inside. "Nice work back there, Paula," he said, lighting her cigarette for her. "Good to know you've still got it."

"I wonder."

"Wonder if you're still got it or if it's good to know you've still got it?" he asked. He was standing a little too close, but Paula was still a pretty lady although she could lose the pixie haircut. Tall, lean, big hazel eyes, high cheekbones; okay, the pixie haircut could stay.

Paula turned and fixed her big hazel eyes on him. "I wonder if it matters, Lowell," she said. "I sang my heart out,

Hackenbush is in there singing her heart out; we spend our lives ripping our guts out and for what? The much vaunted 'moment'? It's not fucking worth it, is it? Well, is it?"

Every once in a while, Lowell wished he was gay. This was one of those times because this kind of weird direct question from a female made his macho, what there was of it, shrivel up, illogical as that might be. "Paula," he said, wondering how he'd sound with a lisp. "You're asking the wrong guy; I'm still out there. Missing you, but I shall console myself with the Hackenbush next week."

"Oh yeah? Where?"

"Oak Room; eight to eleven," he said.

"How civilized."

"What are you doing here tonight, Paula? You haven't been around for years; this is the last place I ever thought I'd run into you," he said, asking the question that had been on his mind since the shock of seeing her again wore off.

"I wanted to see Hackenbush in action," Paula said quietly.

"And?"

"She's pretty good," Paula said coolly. "She's temping for me, you know."

"She is? That must be, ah, interesting," Lowell said. "I heard she was out of work since the Lotus Room was closed, but I didn't realize she'd hit the skids quite so hard."

"There's nothing wrong with working in an office, Lowell."

"Ummm..."

"Well, there's more to it than the Lotus Room, her uke got smashed up."

"I knew that," he said. "I wouldn't ask her to sing for me if she was going lug that terrible thing along."

Paula resisted the irrational urge to defend Hackenbush, who probably didn't need it. "And her car is in the shop," she said. "So, she's temping and I'm damn glad to have her around. She's a good secretary and a calming force in the office."

"Really?"

"Yes, nothing fazes her because it's just a temp job,"

Paula said, stubbing out her cigarette. "She has a unique and refreshing perspective that every office needs."

"Which is?"

"'It's just a day job' kind of attitude," Paula said. "Not good in the long haul, but refreshing in short bursts. Now excuse me, I must go in there and drag my Hackenbushwacked son home before the cops close the place for serving a minor."

"Your baby boy is..."

"Old enough to have a crush on Mabel."

"I don't know which one I feel sorrier for."

"Feel sorry for me, Lowell, I'm his mother and Hackenbush's boss," Paula laughed and went inside.

Lowell followed her in and was amazed at how big the kid, who was a toddler last time he saw him, had gotten. Anyway, he seemed like a good-natured kid because he meekly got up and followed his mother out. On the other hand, Paula had led a few bands in her day and could be a very commanding presence when she wanted to be. And yet, for all her talent, losing her husband had broken her spirit and made her question music. "Pretty women ought not be so complicated," he thought watching Paula thread her way of the crowd and then turned back to watch Hackenbush swooping through *Wave*. For the second time that night Lowell wished he was gay. "Women." Then his eye fell on Shorty. "Men." Maybe he'd just give up on sex entirely and stick to music and flirtation; it was physically and emotionally safer.

At the end of the gig, Cody suggested they go eat at Pipers. Hackenbush missed her band, a lot, and thought this was a good idea. "I dunno know if Luis is into that, he's my ride home, so lemme ask."

It turned out it he wasn't. Much as Luis would have liked to, he never felt safe leaving his bass in his van anywhere, least of all Pipers' parking lot.

Cody came to the rescue and said he'd give her and Shorty a ride home. He lived in Pasadena so it wasn't exactly out of his way. Ross and Gregg were easily persuaded to join them. They missed Hackenbush and Shorty as well. It had been kind of nice watching her sing from the audience, but it was nicer to be behind her with drums or bass or beside her with a guitar.

"Enjoyed your singing tonight, Hackenbush."

Mabel started; she'd been so intent on watching Carlos divvying up the tip jar, she'd not seen Charles come up next to her. Not that she minded Charles being next to her.

"Thanks, very kindly," she said politely. "Paula's got a helluva voice, don't she?"

"Yes, surprising; I had no idea," he said. "Yes, quite different from you though."

"Different better or different worse?"

"Different different," he said, slowly. "I'm not a musician, I'm not sure how to put it. You seem to engage the audience a bit more...somehow."

"Oh, me? I flirt like mad up there, Mr. Withers," she said, pleased he'd been paying attention. "Flirting with a roomful of people is about the safest thing one can do, don't you think?"

"I wouldn't know, Hackenbush," Charles laughed.

"Well, think about it for a second," she insisted. "Flirting with one person, well, that could lead to something more, but flirting with a roomful of people, ha!" She listened to him laugh and was glad he knew that she knew that he knew that she was talking utter nonsense. "Why not come out with us? You and Mr. Withers; it would be fun."

"Well, I–"

"That would be great!" Frank materialized beside them and got directions to Pipers.

Though they were not the largest group in Pipers that night, it did take a few moments to get a table for seven. While they were waiting, Charles asked Hackenbush about the décor, which was red plaid carpet, battle axes on the walls and a suit of armor in the lobby. At Halloween the suit of armor became various spooky impersonations, incredibly topping itself each year, however, now it was only February and therefore it presented a tamer aspect.

"I don't know," she said. "I think it's a Scottish thing. Pipers as in bagpipers, but I've never seen any bagpipes in here so I guess we're supposed to figure it out from the plaid carpet."

"What about the suit of armor?" Frank asked.

"No idea. Guys?" she asked the band and they shook their head. "Who knows? It's been here as long as I can remember."

Their table was ready and Hackenbush took a seat next to Charles, who was studying the menu. "I don't know I've ever seen trout and eggs on a menu before," he murmured.

"Oh! Then I've brought you here just in time!" she murmured back. "Excuse me." Hackenbush leaned over Shorty and had a quick conference with her rhythm section and then waved the waitress over. "We'd like a club sandwich and five forks," she said, after Charles and Frank had ordered.

"Want me to have the cook cut it in six sections like last time?" the waitress asked.

"Excellent. We can arm wrestle for the extra piece."

"Okay," the waitress said, leaving them.

"Hackenbush, I'd like you all to be my guests," Charles said.

"Really?"

"Yes, it would be my pleas–"

"WAITRESS! WAITRESS! PLEASE COME BACK!"

About four seconds of serious meditation on the menu took place before the band ordered their favorite Pipers' dishes, which they usually couldn't afford. Hackenbush ordered steak and eggs.

"A bit late for breakfast, isn't it, Mabel?" Frank asked.

"Your stomach doesn't know what time it is," she said, handing the waitress her menu.

Pipers was jumpin' as usual for that hour on a Sa'day night or Sa'day morning as the case might be. Musicians in various states of exhaustion wandered in, several of them exchanged greetings with Hackenbush or the band. At one point Shorty and Gregg excused themselves to talk to a guy wearing pearls and too much eye-shadow sitting in a booth nearby.

"Somebody you know, Hackenbush?" Charles asked, watching the show.

"Maybe. Seems like I remember that guy sitting with a bunch of clean-cut church-going guys in here a few months ago," she said.

"I remember that," Ross laughed. "What did you call them?"

"Fagelas for Jesus," she said and then had to explain to Charles what a fagela was. "But what I really want to know is why Mr. Macho Guitar Player and Shorty both know the same guy."

Their meals arrived and Shorty and Gregg came back to eat. Charles commented that the food was excellent for coffee shop food. Nobody disagreed.

"So, who's that guy, Gregg?" Hackenbush leaned down the table to ask.

"His name's Bennet," Gregg said.

"Yeah? He's attractive. How'dya know him?"

"Is he?" Frank asked, staring at the guy.

"Yeah, man, I can never get my eye shadow to look that nice." She turned back to Gregg. "So, how'dya know this guy?"

"I went to high school with him," Gregg said.

"Oh." Hackenbush ate her eggs. "What an anti-climax," she though, but asked, "How do you know him, Shorty?"

"Remember the social dancing course I took with Auntie June?" Shorty said.

"The one she paid you by the hour to take with her?" Hackenbush watched him nod. "Yeah, I remember, I also remember not being able to dance with you on far too many nights because of it."

"Gotta get that money where it is, Mabel," Shorty said. "Anyway, that guy there, Bennet, was in the same class. Nice guy; terrible dancer, but that's how it goes."

Mabel flagged the waitress down and asked for more coffee and a doggie bag. She'd take most of her steak home and have it for lunch tomorrow, or rather, today. The waitress brought the bill and Hackenbush watched Charles look it over and lay a five on the table. Hackenbush dug a one and some change out of her bag and put it on the table. She looked up and found Charles smiling at her.

"Am I not leaving enough tip?" he asked.

"Is that twenty-three percent?" she asked.

"No, it's a little over fifteen percent."

"Well, you forgot the eight percent waitress tax," she said, glancing at the bill.

"The what?"

"The waitress tax, it's eight percent on their hourly wages," she explained. "It's a new tax"

"Oh, it's not that new," Shorty said.

"Well, sometime in the past six years, the Feds dreamed up this 'new' tax," she said. "It's supposed to balance the federal budget, but I don't see how since waitresses don't make any money in a place like this anyway. I mean, if the government is so hard up it has to clip waitresses for the tips they might or might not get, then I don't see how eight percent of minimum wage is going to keep us in B-52s or White House china services. Seems unfair to me."

"So if somebody stiffs her for a tip...?" Frank asked.

"She gets penalized another eight percent off the top," Hackenbush said. "And she has to share whatever she does get with the busboys," she added, looking up at Charles, who seemed to be having a debate with himself. She smiled most charmingly when he put a twenty on the table and looked her right in the eye. "You're wonderful," she whispered.

"If you think so, Hackenbush," he said, rising, "then I must be."

While he was paying the bill, the waitress came up to him with the twenty and told him he'd left it on the table. "That's for you, miss, share it with the busboys," Charles blurted.

"Oh, okay," the waitress said, looking at Hackenbush, who just winked and smiled.

"Thank you for supper, Mr. Withers," Hackenbush said politely in the parking lot.

"You're quite welcome, Mabel," Charles said. "May I give you a ride home?"

"Cody has it covered," she said, jerking her chin at the bass player. "But thanks. It would be out of your way anyway."

Charles seemed about to say something, but then just nodded and said good night.

"Not your usual type, Hackenbush," Cody said in the car as they drove up Western.

"What? That guy? He's my boss," she said.

"Oh, yeah? Must be nice to have your boss wrapped around your little finger," he said.

Hackenbush glanced at Shorty, sitting silently in the back seat. He shrugged; no help there. "Well, so, he's nice to me," she said. "He was nice to all of us tonight."

"He's after you, babe."

"So?"

"He's not your type."

"Oh, honestly, Cody. Who the hell is my type these days?"

"Gregg."

"Oh, Christ, Cody! We couldn't get our egos into the same car, let alone the same bed," she laughed.

"You could if you'd settle down, Mabel."

"Oh, pooh," she said, thinking she might be able to settle down but, even if she wanted him, Gregg might not. Besides, Shorty had a crush on Gregg and was making very little headway, but some headway nevertheless. Certainly she didn't want to step on her dance partner's romantic, however futile, toes. "Gregg's too young for me, Cody. He's got too much girl chasing left in his system to settle down with a woman of a certain age like me."

"He likes you, Mabel," Cody said.

"He'd like to fuck me, Cody," she said. "You've been happily married for too long to recognize the signs anymore. You must think everybody wants a cozy home like yours."

"Don't they?"

"Maybe. But right now I just want a good, reliable guitar player in the band and sex would just mess that up," Hackenbush said, suddenly very tired. "D'ya mind if Gregg and I just stay friends? Nice, uncomplicated, gainfully giggin' friends? All of us?"

"Sure, Mabel." Cody smiled and patted her knee. "You wouldn't be living alone if you didn't want to be, I guess."

"Well, yeah, it is keeping me healthy, you know." She listened to him laugh and they rode the rest of the way to her place listening to *Sketches of Spain*.

"Thanks, Cody," she said, getting out of the car and hustling a sleepy Shorty into the house.

They were very tired and didn't waste time on conversation. Being old friends, but modest, they put on their pajamas in different rooms and then got into bed. Hackenbush sat on the edge of the bed to finish her cigarette. She'd left the light on because there was no pleasure for her in smoking in the dark. By that time of night and the twentieth plus cigarette, there was no pleasure left in smoking at all, but the dark just made it worse. "Maybe I should quit," she wondered, glancing down at Shorty, who was not looking at her, but beyond her.

"You still got that picture of Eddy Lee on your nightstand," Shorty said, feeling her gaze. He waved at the tastefully framed picture of Hackenbush and her ex-guitar-player-ex-fiancée in happier days.

"Yeah," Hackenbush said, not looking at it. She stubbed out her cigarette and lay down.

"Y'ever think about him?" He reached across her and turned out the lamp over the photograph.

"Sometimes, Shorty," she said, closing her eyes. "Sometimes I wonder how he's doing, who he's with. Hope he's doing okay, y'know, stuff like that."

"D'you miss him?" Shorty asked, wondering if she was sounding wistful or just tired.

"I dunno know, man, I've felt like this for so long, I can't remember what I was like before. So I don't know if this is missing Eddy or just the way I am now," she said, curling next to him. "Why can't they all be nice, reliable, stick around kinda guys like you, Shorty?"

"Because the species would come to a screaming halt."

"Oh well," she said, sleepily. "That would be one way it could go."

"Hi, Mabel."

"Hi, you," she said, thinking frantically "what's his

name what's his name what's his name?"

"So, can we have lunch today?" Alan asked.

"You bet!" She looked out the window. "Why's this bus so slow today?"

"Accident," he said, pointing at the Jaguar rear-ended by a Mercedes. "Nice cars."

"Yeah, and two body shops just made their payroll this week," she said, thinking this guy, whatever his name, had a cool laugh.

"You look a little tired today," he said.

"I did a fill-in at the Mondrian last night," she said, wondering how tired she looked. "It was a late one and all the way across town, too."

"You did a what?"

"Sorry, Alan," she said, delighted the name just came to her out of the blue. "My pal Ross was playing a casual, a private party, and the singer got the flu, so he called me. Nice gig, too, almost a big band, but not quite."

"What was the party?"

"Wedding reception, I think, some chick dressed-up like a meringue," Mabel said. "She looked way to happy to be dressed-up like that for a human sacrifice, so musta been her wedding."

He laughed again and asked her what time for lunch and where.

Hackenbush was a lot of things, but unnecessarily cruel was not usually one of them. She'd actually given this question some thought when she realized there was no nice way out of lunch with this guy. Her conclusion, based on the way he dressed and his clerk job, was that he didn't have a lot of money. If he took her to La Fonda, which was pricey, she'd want to drink martinis and it would be more pricey still. Same problem with the Sheraton Townhouse and it was quite a schlep from the office. And he seemed like a good-natured guy, so Langers might be in the price range, but getting there through the park could be tricky. The homeless, however harmless, were scary-looking in the daylight and you never knew when you were going to meet an actual mugger and get mugged there. So, having this poor guy escort her diagonally across Macarthur Park was more than either of them could probably handle. That left the Royale or the teriyaki joint in the basement, which didn't have seating and it was raining, so the roof was out for today. There was a rumor of a decent Korean barbecue on Seventh, but she thought she'd stick with the devil she knew for this lunch. "Come get me at noonish," she said, thinking that would impress Paula, who seemed never to go out for lunch. "How about the Royale? They have pretty good lunches."

He said that would be fine and they got off the bus together and went into their days.

Hackenbush ran a little water over her toothbrush and turned off the tap. While brushing she went over the mild-mannered lunch she'd had with Alan. He was nice, had nice manners, a nice laugh and painted toy soldiers in his spare time. That was the most interesting fact she could drag out of him during the entire meal: he had enough energy after an eight hour plus sometimes day to get home and still have whatever it takes to focus down on little tiny metal guys in uniforms. Moreover, he researched the wars so he would know what the uniforms should look like. He did forty-five minutes on the subject and she was damn sure he could probably do twice that in another setting.

"It's like discovering some strange civilization you never even thought existed," she marveled, staring into her eyes and commanding them to unglaze.

Not that Alan was boring, no, quite the reverse; men talking about their passions fascinated Hackenbush, who thought the intensity they put into such things was adorable. And Alan had not done all the talking, by now he knew she was a singer, why and how the Lotus Room got smashed up, why her car was in the shop and, therefore, why she was temping at Withers and Sons.

Hackenbush was rinsing and spitting when Paula breezed up to wash her hands. As courtesy to Paula, she omitted the vigorous tongue brushing her dentist recommend for her smokers' tongue.

"How was your lunch date, Mabel?"

"So so," Hackenbush said. "Nice guy, even though he thinks the album Nelson Riddle did of standards with that country singer... What's her name?"

"Not Willie Nelson?"

"Nah, he's okay; I like that album. Nice version of *Stardust* on it," Hackenbush said. "These are big, huge, gigantic arrangements with those technically impeccable studio musicians. What's her name—Linda...something— anyway, Alan thought that was a great album." She watched Paula shudder like all right-minded good singers. "See? You know what I mean. Let's face it, anyone who could sound bad with those arrangements has more problems than a string section can cure But, Alan, he's a nice guy; not my type, but those are few and far between these days. Maybe I'll introduce him to Adela, ya think?"

"He's not Adela's type either, Hackenbush," Paula said. "You're more Adela's type."

"Huh. I'm flattered, I think." Hackenbush lit a cigarette on the way out of the ladies room. "But does she paint historically accurate tin soldiers, like Alan?"

"I believe she does more decoupage making than tin soldier painting," Paula said, rifling through some paper. "Does he really...?"

"Yes, and talks about it with much fervor!"

"I wish Bobby did that instead of play the guitar."

"Bobby's got music in his blood, Paula," Hackenbush said quietly. "Don't ask birds to swim or fish to live in trees."

"I'm glad you waited until after lunch to deliver that sermonette," Paula said. "Now it will only bother me for half as long." She listened to Hackenbush chuckle. "Mabel, you're a great singer. I've heard people talk about you, but didn't really realize until I heard you. What you have, it's not something you can make words for, you know? You have to hear it to appreciate it."

"Thanks, Paula, that means a lot coming from another diva baby, as Carlos called you later," Hackenbush said.

"Did he?"

"Yes, he was very impressed," Hackenbush said. "So was I," she thought. "So was I," she said.

"Damn Lowell."

"Yeah, what a pain in the ass that guy is," Hackenbush said. "He even told me what to wear to the gig this week."

"Well, it is the Oak Room, Mabel."

"Yeah, and not the Vatican or something. Oh well," Hackenbush said, settling at her desk and putting on the headphones.

The Oak Room was the bar for a very fancy mid-Wilshire restaurant. The restaurant had pale pink walls and was softly lit by chandeliers. An old gigolo once told Hackenbush that women of a certain age were keeping that restaurant in business because, after a certain age, the only thing more flattering than pink walls and soft lights was no light at all. They also served some of the best food in town and lucky Hackenbush would be going an hour early to get hers. Okay, so they made her and Lowell eat in the little staff dining room off the kitchen; the food was too good to rebel about the décor.

The bar, on the other hand, was, as the name implied, paneled in dark-stained oak and had cushy seating that one never wanted to get up from. Hackenbush liked the Oak Room very much; she felt comfortable in there, with the dim lights and dark walls; people in the Oak Room were concentrating on their drinking or the music and not sizing each other up. She'd heard some really fine singing in there and the bartenders made a helluva good Ramos gin fizz.

So, she was leaning on the bar, deep into her first gin fizz, digesting her excellent sole almondine—something she never got enough of, really—when the Withers brothers came in with the Belinda. "Man, there's some sharp edges on that triangle," she thought, listening to Lowell's rather bland rendition of *Misty*, one of the few songs Hackenbush loathed.

Lowell was not the most exciting solo piano player in town, that much was true; he was good for a low-key, high-tone room like this one. He was, however, one of the best accompanists in town and knew it. All the singers knew it, too, so the invitation to sing for him at the Oak Room was quite a compliment to Mabel. And, further, all the singers knew not to mess with Lowell because he'd accompany you into hell and then leave you there. So singers toed the line, sang the song, and saved the wilder flights of fancy for the jazz gigs. Lowell had already informed her that they would be performing *Stardust*, *Stormy Weather*, *My Funny Valentine* (another least liked song, unless she could swing it), *How Long Has This Been Going On?*, and anything else he told her to sing THE WAY IT WAS ORIGINALLY COMPOSED.

"Ah, Lowell, you're no fun anymore," she'd said.

"And wear the simplest black dress you own," he had added. "And no spandex; it's the Oak Room."

So Hackenbush stood at the bar looking forward to doing some very pure singing over the next four nights. Well, there must be some good in these songs without frills or they wouldn't still be around; of course the only reason they were still around is because they were frill-able, but that was another matter. She'd taken Lowell seriously on the dress as well as the music.

Long ago, Hackenbush lost a bet—she couldn't even remember what the bet had been about—and wound up singing art songs in a Pasadena wine bar accompanied by a lute-playing Jet Propulsion Laboratory rocket scientist. It was a nightmare at the time because that kind of singing was hard work for her. Vocally, it required more control and no fooling around with the song. So, it was harder than belting a standard or dancing with Shorty; she had to concentrate. For these gigs, she'd picked up a very simple black silk jersey, scoop-necked, floor-length, A-line dress that was flattering, chic, modest, and gave her room to expand her ribcage without looking like a freak.

"That table is picking up your and Lowell's tab tonight."

Hackenbush started; she was so deep in her reverie, she'd not noticed Drusilla the bartender, come up beside her. She smiled and sketched a wave at the trainwre– um, trio at the table. "They'd like you to sit with them if you're so inclined."

"Can you please tell them I'm too nervous before the first song to be much fun and I'll come over on the break?"

"Will do, lady."

"Anything you want to hear tonight, Dru?" Hackenbush asked, leaning over the bar, watching her make cocktails. 'That neat scotch must be for Charles,' she thought.

"How about *I'm Beginning To See The Light?*"

"I'll see if I can get Lowell to do that one; he might consider it too rousing for the Oak Room." Hackenbush listened to Drusilla's polite laugh. "What's your second choice?"

"*Lush Life* or *Body And Soul.*"

"Ah, brutes of songs, but sufficiently dirge-like for Mr. Lowell to approve of." And just at that particular moment, Mr. Lowell was introducing her:

"Ladies and Gentlemen, we have an exceptional treat tonight," he was saying. "I succeeded in luring one of the finest singers in Los Angeles to the Oak Room for a few days and I hope you enjoy her as much as audiences all over town have. Ladies and Gentlemen, please welcome, direct from the middle class, the fabulous Dr. Hackenbush!"

Gliding up to the stand, Mabel gave Lowell a grateful smile; she hadn't thought he'd use her hipster introduction, but he had and therefore went up a few notches in her esteem.

Hackenbush adjusted her mike, smiled at Charles, and noticed Paula slipping into a seat in the darkest corner of the bar wearing dark glasses. "I see you, Dreisler," she thought, jerking her chin at the office manager while Lowell cruised them into *Let's Face The Music And Dance*; lyrics to live by, really.

Whatever protective deity that looks after singers and their pianists was on the job that night; Hackenbush and Lowell's chemistry was perfect and the music was damn close to perfect. They were definitely on the same wavelength; Hackenbush felt comfy enough to put a few frills in and Lowell even used them in his solo. Things got a little vague in *Body And Soul*, but Lowell segued right into *Stardust*, Hackenbush's talisman song, and they were right back in the groove. Feeling benevolent, Lowell even took a chance on *I'm Beginning To See The Light* for Drusilla and it played like a dream; a happy dream. Lowell announced a break and gave Hackenbush's hand a warm squeeze as he led her off the stand. "See how good you can be when you behave yourself?" he asked.

"Let's do *Lady Be Good* next set and find out, hey?"

"Anything you want, Doc."

They separated; Hackenbush to sit with the fascinating Withers brothers and whatzername, Belinda; yeah, Belinda. Lowell joined Paula at her table. "I wonder if you can damage your eyes wearing dark glasses at night?" he asked. She took them off. "Much better, your eyes are too beautiful to hide, Paula."

"Why, Lowell!"

"Oh, don't mind me; I'm falling in love with Hackenbush tonight," he said, accepting a drink from Drusilla. "I'm hoping she won't do anything to break the spell, but I know she will."

"She'd hardly be Hackenbush if she didn't," Paula said, digging her credit card out of her purse and holding it out to Drusilla. "Just enjoy it while it lasts."

"Hackenbush's party is taking care of your tab, ma'am," Drusilla said. "You, too, Mr. Lowell."

"How nice of them," Lowell murmured to Drusilla's back. "'Hackenbush's party'? What's that about?"

"Those two guys are partners in the law firm I work at–"

"Where Mabel is temping?"

"Yes, and she fascinates them."

"Oh, I can see that," Lowell said, watching Hackenbush gesture theatrically and smile a little too brightly. His good feelings about her went back to normal; she could sing, but she was also a big pain in the neck. He looked over at Paula watching the scene, too.

"Lord, I can remember striking those poses, over and over and over, until I got married," she said with a wistful smile. "Thank God that's all over for me."

"Seems like it's all over for Hackenbush, too," Lowell murmured. "It's been four years since Eddy Lee dumped her and I hear there's no one new."

"How about you?"

"Me and Hackenbush? I'd rather sleep on concrete than deal with that ego," Lowell laughed.

"Well, okay, not you. But four years is too long, she ought to get over it and find someone new."

"Like you did?"

"I don't want anybody else." Paula looked into her drink.

"So, maybe Mabel feels the same."

"It's not the same thing, Lowell; my man is dead."

"Yeah and at least you know where your man is, Paula. Hackenbush has the extra torment of wondering," Lowell said.

"Yeah and at least Hackenbush might, maybe someday might see Eddy Lee again."

"And how awful would that be after the way he dumped her?"

Paula opened her mouth and closed it. She glanced at the Withers table. "I've no idea, Lowell; Hackenbush is looking at her watch."

Lowell looked at his watch and said, "It's that time," he said, getting up. "Do you hate me or may I come back on the next break?"

"Sure, Lowell," Paula said warmly. "No hard feelings. I might have to leave though; it's a work night."

"Well, stick around for at least one more song, okay?"

"Okay."

Lowell caught up with Hackenbush, drifting toward the piano.

"Let's do–" Hackenbush began.

He took her by the arm and snapped, "Sing *How About Me?*"

"Why would you want to hear that maudlin–?"

"Just sing it like you mean it."

"Is anything else possible with those words?"

"Just sing, Mabel."

And she did.

Charles and Belinda left midway through the third set, but Frank stayed to the very end. "Can I give you a lift home, Mabel?" he asked while Lowell was packing up.

"No thanks, Mr. Withers, Lo–"

"Frank, please."

"No thanks, Frank; Lowell has it covered," she said, lighting up. "He lives out that way."

"It wouldn't be out of my way, wherever you live."

"Where do you live, Frank?"

"The Marina."

"Thanks, but no thanks, Frank," she said as Lowell steered her to the door. "I'll see you at the office tomorrow."

"I really need to talk to you," Frank said, following them to Lowell's fuel-efficient Japanese car.

Hackenbush rolled down the window. "Tomorrow, Frank, honest. Hey, look out!" She waved as Lowell roared out of the parking lot.

"He seemed like a nice guy," Lowell said a couple of blocks down Wilshire.

"I guess."

"This is what's wrong with you, Hackenbush, you're indifferent to men."

"What?"

"You heard me."

"What's it to ya, Lowell?" she asked, tossing her smoke out the window. "Anyway, I wouldn't be indifferent to the right man."

"How right has a guy got to be to get you to consider him?"

"Why, Lowell!"

"Not me, you idiot; I'm talking about that guy back there. What's his name...?"

"Frank."

"Yeah; Frank."

"He doesn't want me."

"If you'd just open your eyes–"

"No, Lowell, believe me; my eyes are wide open on this one. Frank is in love with his brother's girlfriend," Hackenbush said. "That emaciated and anemic washed out-lookin' blonde they were sitting with is the object of his desire."

At the next light, Lowell turned to get a good look at her. "Are you making this up?"

"Lowell," she said. "Not even I could make that up."

The rest of the way to Casa Hackenbush, they talked about music, which was a much safer subject than sex, let alone love.

"Mabel, I have to talk to you!" Frank hissed the second she sat down at her desk.

"Buy me lunch and you can talk all you want," she hissed back, changing from canvas slip-on shoes to closed-toed pumps with modest heels.

"Okay. Where?"

"Langers." She watched him walk away thinking he'd be amusing in Macarthur Park and also that she'd like to save LaFonda for a lunch she might really enjoy. Like a nice cozy lunch with Paula to find out what Lowell's fucking problem was and/or to talk about music. Hackenbush was of the opinion that you could never talk too much about music and never have too many people around to talk about it to. However, today she was having lunch with Frank at Langers, if they made it across the park.

"So far so good," she thought, eyeing some hard-looking characters lounging by the duck-less lake. She noticed Frank was being watchful, too, and she wondered if there was any benefit in having him with her. "Ten o'clock, Frank," she murmured, not making eye contact with the guy slanting across the grass at them.

"Hey, man and lady, you got some change so I can get something to eat?"

"I only have a twenty," Frank said, handing it over under Mabel's shocked eyes. "And you're my bodyguard now. I'll be coming back this way in about an hour; I want you to make sure I make it. Understand."

"Yeah, man; thanks!"

"What are the chances of him being anywhere near here with that twenty to protect you in an hour, Frank?" Mabel asked when she figured they were out of the guy's hearing.

"Have more faith, Mabel."

"Oh, I'll work on that, Frank." She rolled her eyes. However, she did notice a few raggedy-looking men and women approach them and then veer off, but didn't have the balls to look behind her. "I dunno, Frank, seems like you just told the whole park you're mugging material."

"Or I just told them not to mess with my bodyguard," he said, holding open Langers Deli's door for her.

"Thanks. Does your brother get to Langers the same way?" she asked, scanning the busy restaurant for a seat.

"Charles never comes to Langers," Frank said, steering her to the table a harried waitress waved him to. "He's more of a Greenblatts Deli man. However, if he wants Langers, he orders it over the phone and then lends Bobby his car. A waitress then runs out to the curb with the food and gets the money. Very efficient; I've done that myself."

"Borrowed Charles's car?" she asked, uselessly perusing the menu since she always got the same thing there.

"No, lent Bobby mine."

They both ordered pastrami on rye; Frank ordered one to go.

"Who's that for?" she asked, sipping her coffee. Langers made really good coffee.

"My bodyguard," he said.

"Ever the optimist, aren't you, Frank?" She rolled her eyes again and decided that was enough eye-rolling for one lunch.

"I'm trying to impress you because I need your help. I—"

Hackenbush held up a hand. "Please! Let me enjoy some pastrami before you ask me to do something and I say no."

"Oh, you'll like this," he assured her, but did wait until she'd eaten half her sandwich before he continued: "I want you to seduce Charles away from Belinda."

"No."

"Why not? He likes you; you like him. I can tell."

"Because, Frank, there's a lyric in *Harlem Gin Blues* that I have made my motto to live by and stay healthy with," she said, slathering a little more mustard on her rye. "And it is, 'Blues and Trouble go 'round hand in hand, but you ain't had no trouble 'til you mess with Another Woman's Man'. I like you, Frank, I even like your brother, but truer words were never sung by so many women, and a few men, and I'm not about to—"

"I love her."

"You're stupid; she's with Charles."

"She loves me."

"She's stupid; she's with Charles."

"She's afraid to leave him."

"Why? Is he going to beat you both up?"

"I don't think so. She's afraid of what people will think if she leaves him for me," Frank said, as if Hackenbush could understand this.

"People will think she prefers you to him," she said, frowning at her huge pastrami sandwich and then asking for a to go container. "People, women, children, even pets, change their minds when they see a better deal. Why not Belinda? This is Amurrica; where each and every one of us has the right in this democratic nation to change our minds and get a different man or whatever if that's the desired thang." She looked up at the waitress, shoveling her half sandwich into the Styrofoam. "Thanks; how many times have you changed your mind this week, miss?" she asked.

"Eleven," the harried woman said, gently slamming their check on the table.

"Is it fifteen plus eight or do you round up to twenty-five percent for the tip?" Frank asked, studying the bill.

"I round up to twenty-five." She lit a cigarette and sighed out a lungful of smoke. "Okay, tell me about you and Belinda," she said, leaning her elbows on the table and mentally lining up a salt mine to take it with.

Later on, back in the office, Hackenbush was recovering from Frank's long, sad story as well as the return trip across the park. As she predicted, Frank's new bodyguard was nowhere to be seen, but a new guy was willing to take over for the pastrami sandwich and a five. Most of this transaction was lost on Hackenbush as she was deep in thought about what a mess Frank and Belinda were making for themselves because they were both cowards. Spoiled, gutless, useless cowards, if she wanted more adjectives. And she did want more adjectives; she wanted to beat those two over the head with all the syntax she could muster.

The scene was pretty simple: Frank had met Belinda at

UCLA where she was studying something like medieval French poetry and writing papers on why a bunch of dead incomprehensible French troubadours were crucial to whatever she had to say about them, and somebody ought to tell her she was wasting her time (at least Mabel Hackenbush was unimpressed) and UCLA's resources, but then again, UCLA could probably use all the carriage trade, full-tuition-in-cash types they could get, however silly their major. Aren't there already enough or too many medievalists out there as it is? So, anyway, in the course of courting this fine young thing, Frank makes the mistake of introducing her to his father and brother. Unfortunately, for Frank, Charles's eye falls favorably upon the lass and he begins to be charming in a very direct and meaningful manner. Thus causing Hackenbush to wonder what else Charles took away from his younger brother just to prove he could.

Possibly Withers Senior helped out by making a call to Evil Big Daddy Rafeson, because Evil Big Daddy Rafeson evidently told his lovely child to hook the heir to the Withers fortune if she could. Although the Rafesons were really quite rich, they were not as rich as the Withers clan and they were a bit more respectable for being patrons of the arts and sciences. But, oh, the snobbisma; they had tasteful concert halls, well stocked galleries and state of the art laboratories named after them on the East Coast and the California branch of the family was only out west due to a beloved child's asthma in the 1950s. Well, this stem never left the sunny coast and lived quietly on their Malibu hacienda or their other beach 'cottage' (trans. mansion) in Santa Barbara. However, the family feeling must have been, if their girl could catch a Withers (who were obscenely rich and politically well connected, if rather eccentric), especially the legitimate one, then she should.

And, much to love-struck Frank's horror, she did. Belinda had merely told him that her 'relationship' with Charles, as she called it, didn't mean she had to stop seeing him...in private. To her credit, she more honestly admitted later that she simply didn't have the courage to go against her family's wishes. Unless Charles did something outrageous, she had said, she would marry him if and when he asked her.

"And running around with me is outrageous enough for her to grow a spine and dump him for you?" Hackenbush had asked.

"Yes," Frank had said. "Belinda said especially if you become a public embarrassment."

"Oh, I see; Belinda is in on this scam, too."

"Yes, that's why she came to the Oak Room last night; she wanted a better look at you."

"Oh, I see; am I embarrassing enough for her?"

"Yes."

So, sitting at her desk, Hackenbush had merely said she'd think about vamping Charles in her copious spare time for his and Belinda's benefit, while silently vowing that wild horses could not–

"Enjoyed your singing last night."

Hackenbush looked up at the very much and very easily maligned Charles and said, very nicely, "Thank you. Come back if you want to; I'm there through Saturday."

"I'll do my best," he said, handing her some dictation cassettes. Well, at least it took her mind off Frank's twisty-wisty idea.

That night, she told the whole thing to Shorty over the phone. He was on a new house-sitting gig for the next two months and was happy as a shrimp cocktail. "I mean, Shorty, I've spent my life trying to avoid useless, ruthless, creepy people like the Withers clan and here I am, plunked down in a nest of them and one of them is asking me to do his evil bidding."

"Are you gonna?"

"No! I wouldn't know where to begin. I am not now nor have I ever been much of a vamp, you know."

"Oh, I know. I also know that Charles guy does have his eye on you, so you really wouldn't have to work to hard to–"

"Shorty! I'm not getting involved with this guy!"

"Why not?"

"Because I... Have you heard a word I've said?"

"Well, not really, I've been trying to program the VCR."

Hackenbush had a momentary urge to slam the phone

down in his masculine little ear, but decided to laugh instead. The temp gig was up in two weeks, her car would be ready, the Lotus Room would be open, hopefully she'd be back there or somewhere just as nice with her lovely new baritone ukeuele. Life would be beautiful as long as she didn't get sucked into the Withers mess. Oh well.

Charles never turned up at the Oak Room again that week, but Belinda did near the end of the last set that Friday. Wearing dark glasses, she scuttled in and took the darkest seat in the back she could find. She even blew out the candle.

"Mata Hari in the corner over there wants to talk to you," Drusilla told Hackenbush, tilting her chin at the darkness.

"I can just make out the blond hair," Hackenbush murmured. "Any idea what she wants?"

"No, but she was drinking Piña Coladas the first night she was in here and now she's on neat vodka, her third, and that can't be good; she's too thin to drink like that." Drusilla, like Wang, was one of the great and wise bartenders of Los Angeles.

"What's up?" Shorty joined them. With his house-sitting client's permission, he was out on the town in their car that evening. He and Hackenbush were going to hear some music in Glendale and visit some of their old haunts.

"Dunno; let's go find out," she said leading him over to Belinda. "So... Belinda, to what do I owe the honor...?"

"Who is that?" the blond asked in a scared voice.

"A friend; calm down." Hackenbush pulled out a chair for Shorty and one for herself. Once her eyes adjusted to the deep gloom, she'd gotten a good look at Belinda and been somewhat alarmed by the hunted, haunted and exhausted expression on her. "No wonder she's sitting in the dark; she looks like shit," Hackenbush thought, but asked, "What's up?"

"Charles proposed yesterday."

"And you said...?"

"I said, yes, and then I didn't sleep all night..."

"Good not sleeping with somebody else in the bed or not sleeping alone?" Shorty asked.

"Alone..."

"What a romantic guy Charles is," Hackenbush thought.

"...after Charles left, that is..."

"Ah. Well, congratulations and good-night, we have–" Hackenbush began.

"And then tonight Frank came over," Belinda went on. "His brother or father told him Charles and I are engaged. He was hysterical, I was hysterical, and then he left in a rage."

"Well, that's too bad, I try to avoid hysterics and rage, my own and others, as much as possible," Hackenbush said, briskly. "Thanks for coming by to tell me this, sister, I'm sure–"

"Mabel, I know you think we're nuts and you've no reason to help me." Belinda took a deep breath. "But can you please at least help me find Frank, please? You're the only one who can help me and–"

"What about your fiancé, Charles?"

Belinda deflated. "I'm not a strong person; I don't think I could stand what would happen...and I don't think I can stand seeing Frank humiliated any more..." She began to cry in a very well-bred way.

Hackenbush hated anybody's tears, however stupid they seemed to her. "Okay, where do you think he is?" she asked. She glanced at Shorty to see if he was looking disgusted, but he just seemed sorry to see a lady crying and was taking notes on a napkin. "My guy Friday," she thought.

"I can't believe we're taking our night out to look for Frank," Hackenbush said in the car.

"It's our good deed."

"Yeah, yeah, yeah." They had a general location of some nasty mid-city bars and Belinda's address in Beverly Glen, whither they should deliver whatever they could find of Withers Other. "I really didn't want to get involved in this."

"Think of it as just doing one little favor so you don't have to do the big one," Shorty said, looking for parking. "I mean, wouldn't you rather do this than seduce your boss?"

"You're right," she agreed, getting out of the car. "Seducing my boss would be way too much fun compared to this. Gotta keep the suffering level up, you know. Hmmmm."

Hackenbush peered into one of the dim, grimy joints and wrinkled her nose.

"See him?"

"No, but I can't see anyone else either." She sighed and hoped these bar patrons would believe they were just looking for someone and not for trouble. "This is the kind of place that ox that thrashed the Lotus room would be in."

"Please, Mabel, this is scary enough."

It was not in that bar or the next one, but in the third one they found Frank. He was half passed out over a table, muttering incoherently and shaking his fist at nothing in particular.

"This," Shorty gestured at Frank, "is what that skinny girl was crying about?"

"Yes. Ain't love grand? He does look better standing up and conscious, I will say that." She noticed the bartender waving them over. "Yes, my fine young thing?"

"Hey lady, you know that guy?" the kid bartender asked.

"Not well, but enough to get him home. What's it to ya, sonny?"

"Well, he was flashin' a lotta green in the process of getting blitzed, ya know? And he left his wallet on the bar." The kid held it up for her to see. "I put it here for safe-keeping until it was last call and I could get the guy a cab somewhere. Got his car keys, too. If you can tell me who it says he is on his license, I'll hand over both and he's all yours."

"Frank Withers, address is somewhere over in the Marina," she said, thinking this kid had the makings of a great bartender or humanitarian or both.

"Isn't that what Bukowski named his daughter? Otherwise, I wouldn't know the Marina if it bit me on the ass," he said, handing her the wallet and a matching wallet of keys. "Your Frank seems all ripped up about a chick."

"Yeah, disgusting, ain't it?" Hackenbush handed him one of her cards. "Call me if you ever want a bartending job in a better neighborhood. No promises, but I have a few connections."

"And leave all this?" he asked, waving his skinny arms

around.

Hackenbush let him have the last word and went to the table to collect the Frank. "You know, I don't know what Frank drives," she said, looking at the keys.

"Looks like a BMW to me, lady," a big burly guy said over her shoulder. "Won't be hard to find around here."

"If it is still around here," she said. "I don't suppose you could give us a hand?"

The guy looked over Hackenbush in her evening gown and Shorty in his amusing little suit that Winnie the Pooh might have worn had he taken up a career in banking. He obviously decided to do a good deed, because he handed his cue to another guy and slung Frank over his shoulder. "Let's go."

They were able to find Frank's car not too far from the joint and poured him into the back seat. Hackenbush handed the burly guy her card and said if he ever came to hear her sing, she'd buy him a drink or two. He said he'd do the best he could to come hear her sing. She and Shorty thanked him profusely and hoped he would.

Hackenbush followed Shorty to Belinda's place in Frank's BMW. After all, if he was going to wake up and puke, it should be in his own car. No such thing happened and pretty soon they were walking him up to Belinda's door.

"Oh my God!" Belinda rushed out to help them walk-carry him inside. "Oh my–"

"Hush, honey, he's alright; just needs a place to sleep it off," Shorty hissed at her.

She led them into her bedroom and they dropped Frank on the coverlet. He was her problem now.

"Hackenbush..." Belinda began.

"Yesssss?"

"I know you think we're foolish, this thing with me and Frank and Charles..." she watched Hackenbush nod vigorously. "But if you could help us...the way Frank told you...I..."

"I just did help you," Hackenbush said, waving Shorty back into the night. "As much as I'm gonna help you, Belinda. Because unless you grow a spine, you're marrying

Charles for his money and breaking Frank's heart for kicks. Good-night."

"You don't know the trouble money causes," Belinda sighed.

"Hey lady, you're right! I only know the trouble of trying to stay middle class," she snarled. "Even in the lower end of it."

"That wasn't very nice," Shorty said in the car.

"I'm pissed off." Hackenbush lit a cigarette. "These fuckers want it all their own way; no struggle, no sacrifices, no tough decisions. They just want it to fall in their laps, the bastards, and when it won't, call in the fucking maid to clean up the mess. I'm not the fucking maid, Shorty."

"No, I see you more as the fucking secretary."

Hackenbush choked on a lungful of smoke. "Y'know, Shorty, I must be losing my touch," she said when she could. "I can't tell the difference between love and obsession anymore."

"There's a difference?"

"That's what they tell me," she said and suggested they go to the Doric Bar, which was unfashionable, but busy, put some Basie on the jukebox and dance for a while.

They danced until closing and then went to Pipers, where they ran into some people who knew of a party at somebody's house on Wilton near Beverly. Good thing for Hackenbush the next day was Saturday because she didn't get home until well after dawn.

On Tuesday, Carlos called her with a casual for Sa'day, March twelfth. Hackenbush looked at her calendar and said she was free that particular Saturday and would be delighted.

"Wear something tight, diva baby, and bring Shorty," Carlos wheezed over the phone.

"Does he get paid? It's a casual, Carlos; no tips."

"Yes, diva, the caterer specifically asked for you and Shorty and as much of your orchestra I could get," Carlos said. "Without you, there is no gig."

"Huh, well; what's it pay?"

"Two hundred each, for Shorty as well."

Hackenbush took a moment to be pleased with that arrangement and then went back to business. "Whose PA?" she asked.

"The caterer will provide."

Hackenbush would bring her own mike, like she usually did, but had no objection to other people's public address systems. She got the time and location—Hancock Park—and just then was merely glad it wasn't too far from home. She thanked Carlos and went back to work.

There was actually a lot of work to do since Hackenbush had left at a normal hour most of last week for the Oak Room gig. Well, that was over and it was back to go like hell.

Charles was working right along with her, and documents were flying between them so there was no room for sparks or smoldering looks. Not that Hackenbush was up for that anyway as she still believed that another woman's man was the worst kind of trouble. And this guy, if she continued to think about it, was attractive in a sober suit-wearing kind of way, but that was about it. She'd probably rather bank with him than sleep with him. He probably didn't even own a leather jacket; no common ground at all.

Opposites attract? Well, that was bullshit, okay, maybe they attract for a couple of hours or a sweaty weekend, but in the long run, one of them has to change a lot and then how opposite is that?

A little after nine, Charles told her to go home unless she wanted some Scotch. "Ah, my chance to escape," she thought, but decided to have some Scotch anyway. If it was the same Scotch as last time she might have a lot since it was very good stuff, otherwise she would have one drink to be polite and then go home.

"You were different at the Oak Room," he said, pouring out their drinks neat. "Very good, but somehow more..."

"Subdued?" she asked, tasting her drink. It was the same Scotch; she would be here awhile. "That's almost de rigueur for places like the Oak Room. Not too much hopping around, no swearing and heaven forbid you sing with anything resembling passion. It ruins people's digestion and they don't drink as well."

"I wonder if passion isn't overrated."

"It depends on what you have to go with it," she said. "Sometimes all people have is their passion for music, art–"

"Oh, I was thinking about sex."

"Sex, money, revenge," she said, wondering where this conversation heading. "It's a big subject: is it passion or lust? Or rage? Does it burn itself out? Or become a passion for something else?"

"Good questions, Hackenbush."

"And how often is passion mistaken for love or control?" she asked, pushing her glass forward for a refill. "And how often are greed and hatred veiled as a 'passionate commitment' to a cause?"

"Do you have any 'passionate commitments' to any causes, Hackenbush?"

"No. I just want to sing and have fun and live and let live; too bad Ronald Reagan hates me and George Bush hates me more. At least Reagan is still acting, even though it's performance art now; gotta give him a little credit for staying in the entertainment field."

"Hate is a pretty strong word," Charles said, pouring for both of them and leaning back. "Are you sure they've even noticed you?"

"Sure they have," she said, enjoying her Scotch and lighting, or trying to light a cigarette with a dead disposable lighter. Charles leaned over his desk and lit it for her. "I don't fit into their world view. I've never voted for Reagan and I'm not rich white guy."

"Oh, come now."

"Really, Mr. Withers, I'm–"

"Call me Charles."

"Okay. Really, Charles, what has Reagan ever done for me? Nothing."

"Well, what has he done to you?"

"Well, he's interfering with my sex life."

"I beg your pardon?"

"Yup, Ronald Reagan has wrecked my sex life because he won't admit there's an AIDS epidemic and rally the country to combat it," she said. "Or whatever Presidents do when they're forced to admit they have a national emergency that they don't like on their hands."

"I see."

"Secondly, I don't believe anyone who will never get an abortion should be for or against it; frankly, it's none of male-type mens' business."

"So the Supreme Court full of men had no business ruling on Roe vs. Wade?"

"Touché, Charles!" Hackenbush sipped her drink. "Of course they did; it's their job. And an excellent job they did: let abortion be legal; let women choose to bring a child to term or not; let every child be a wanted child. You know, I never want to have an abortion, but I'd like to know I can get one if I need one. I mean, everybody has a bad day or slips up now and then."

"Ah, but the AIDS epidemic has solved both your problems, Hackenbush: what can be safer than safe sex?"

"No sex."

"Hmmmm. Sounds like living death."

"Nah, living death is dying at County Hospital of AIDS or trying to raise a kid on our ridiculous minimum wage and no health insurance," she said quietly. "No sex is a cake walk compared to those struggles."

"And this is all Ronald Reagan's fault?"

"Yup; and his friends' fault, too. I'm not saying he did it alone; he has Nancy to help him and all those right-wing Republican types who think if the rich get richer something other than the rich getting richer will happen."

"A rising tide raises all boats, Hackenbush."

"I suppose it depends on the boat," she said. "And if one even has a boat in the first place."

"Reagan's all right," Charles said, pouring for them again. "We needed strong leadership after the Carter years."

"Oh? Do we really need someone to distract us with the 'Evil Empire' when we have so many problems here? Many of them even more evil than the Soviet Union. Why go looking for trouble elsewhere?"

"Our national morale was eroded under Carter."

"Only because we were beginning to see ourselves in the

world," she said. "Reagan got elected to tell the insecure conservatives how wonderful the US is. I'm not saying we're not wonderful, after all, the US is like most people I know: good-looking and talented, but broke, in debt and no healthcare coverage." She listened to Charles laugh and was glad the tension was breaking up. "One more drink and I go home," she thought, but said, "A wise man once told me that true patriotism was seeing your country for what it is, warts and all, and still loving it enough to do whatever you can to make it a better place for everyone. No matter how unpopular that makes you at cocktail parties. I still believe that."

"You can't save the world, Hackenbush."

"And nobody wants me to, least of all me. I just want the rights and freedoms and equality I was raised to believe in to still exist, for everyone, not just for those who can afford them. Well, thanks for the Scotch and the soapbox; it's late and I should be going." She finished her drink.

"Yes, it's late," Charles said. "I asked you to have a drink to help me celebrate my engagement, but we got distracted by our political differences."

"Ah, well, one more drink to your engagement can't hurt," she said, shoving her glass at him. When it was full, she raised it in a toast and wished him many years of happiness, secretly knowing that probably wasn't going to happen, but it was none of her business anyway.

"I do like hearing your politics, Hackenbush; you're the only dissenting voice around me these days."

"Oh, I guess I am dissenting," she said. "But I don't think we're that different politically. I just want the government to do all the stuff that keeps the country going and stay out of my face."

"I'm with you there."

"I don't even want to be in the mainstream, I–"

"No fame? No fortune?"

"Oh, I'd love it, if I could still dance with Shorty and sing with my band," she said. "But mostly I just want to have my life and mind my own business."

"What's stopping you?"

"The Reagan Revolution. Devolution, I think it's called.

I call it gutting the government agencies that help and protect everyone, including rich people, but especially the poor. I mean, money can buy clean air and water, decent housing, healthcare, art, safe streets if you have that kind of money. But the rest of us, most of us, in fact, just do not matter to this administration. And we don't have any money for clean air and water and all that stuff. We're broke and not even a blip on the Reagan/Bush radar. Maybe that's not hatred; it's worse, it's annihilation through indifference. And that seems very wrong to me in a great and democratic country like ours. But we're back on politics, Charles, how does that happen?"

"It's a big subject," he said vaguely.

"Well, I hope you and Belinda will be very happy."

"How did you know I was marrying Belinda?"

"Frank told me at lunch last week that you and she were quite serious," Hackenbush said, carefully skimming along the safer part of the truth. "I just assumed it was her."

"Correctly assumed."

"Well, I hope you'll be happy."

"I think we will be."

"Well, that's good."

"Belinda and I are very similar."

"Well, that's good."

"In our backgrounds and outlook on life."

"Well, that's good."

"We care about the same things."

"Well, that's good."

"Her family is a little eccentric."

"Well, that's good."

"Is it?"

"Wouldn't it be boring if you were exactly the same?"

"Ah; I see. For example, her mother had no interest in arranging the engagement party; my father and Suzy are handling it," he said. "By the way, Suzy Reed is one of the best things that's happened to us lately; thank you for that, Hackenbush."

"Oh, you're welcome."

"I asked her to book you and Carlos for the party."

"Oh, so that's the job on the twelfth," Hackenbush said,

feeling torn between gratitude and attitude. "Thank you, we can always use the work, you know. When we have the time, that is."

"Well, that's good," he said and smiled at her.

"Yeah, well, thanks for the drinks; good night." Hackenbush gathered up her things, called a cab and went down to lobby. "Hi, Walter."

"Hello, Dr. Hackenbush," he said.

"Ah ha, you found out about me!"

"I did; I saw a notice in the paper that you were singing somewhere." He beamed at her. "I never knew you were a singer."

"I am when I'm not a worn-out temp secretary," she said, peering in to the lobby shadows, trying to discern any shapes there. "Want me to prove it?"

"Sure."

She sang *Let's Call a Heart a Heart* until her taxi came and never knowing if she had an audience of more than Walter, she put her whole heart into it, like she always did.

When she got home there was a message on her machine from her father's latest girlfriend telling Hackenbush that her father was dying, so she better come down tomorrow. She better call and find out what was truly up before she made any plans.

"He's that bad, um..." Hackenbush totally blanked on the woman's name and then remembered, "Sheila?"

Apparently so; Sheila told her what nursing home he was in and hung up. Hackenbush wondered if she'd ever meet Sheila in person since it didn't sound like she was going to stick around any longer than any of the other women in her father's life.

She called Anna and told her she wouldn't be at Withers and Sons the next day and why.

"Anything I can do, Hackenbush?" Anna asked.

"Nah, just tell them I had to go visit my poor old daddy at the nursing home and I'll be back on Thursday," Mabel said.

Anna said she would and Hackenbush knew she would. Her next call was to Amtrak to find out about the southbound train, the San Diegan, she thought it was called. And then she went to bed and didn't sleep very well.

The next morning Hackenbush took the bus down to Union Station and got on the southbound train. It would drop her in Santa Ana and then she'd spend some hard-earned cash on a cab to the nursing home.

Waiting for the train to leave, she thought about her dad: the fabulous Louis Hackenbush. It was an unusual chore for her because over the past twelve years, since she'd moved to LA, there hadn't been much to think about. They weren't close, they didn't seek each other out and they'd only worked together about a dozen times in their lives. Okay, so he gave her her first baritone ukulele; he'd won it in a card game and in a boozy burst of fatherly affection decided to give it to his little girl. Sober, he'd tried, unsuccessfully, to take it away from his little girl.

"If you're gonna fight for something that hard, doc, you better make sure it's worth it," he'd said.

It was a threat and even at the tender age of six, Mabel Hackenbush knew a threat when she heard one. Many years later she realized it was more of a challenge, but it was all water under the bridge by then. Fortunately, at that time, her mother hadn't left them yet and when she found a second hand ukulele book at the St. Vincent de Paul Society thrift shop, she gave it to Mabel. The book was for a regular or soprano ukulele, but even as a kid, Mabel had a great ear and could figure the chords out. Very soon she was playing along with her father's favorite Billie Holliday albums. And singing; she had a weak kid voice and the uke is a soft instrument so they were hand in glove. Her mother was delighted and began to teach Mabel to play the piano, even taught her to read music. Five years later, when her mother had gotten fed up with living with an unreliable jazz musician and left, Mabel was playing well enough to keep learning on her own.

Her father was useless to her; he either spoiled her or ignored her. For a few months after her mother left, he was lonely enough to play duets with Mabel and teach her new songs. He'd play the clarinet, she'd play her ukulele and sing whatever he wanted to hear. Their favorite songs were *When You're Smiling* and *Pennies From Heaven*. The musical interlude only lasted until the first girlfriend moved in and then Mabel pretty much kept to herself. When that relationship broke up, there'd be music again, until the next woman took up temporary residence.

This was the usual pattern. The last time she'd seen her father was in November, before Sheila arrived. He'd been diagnosed with lung cancer in October and his girlfriend-up-till-then had blown. How her old cancer-ridden daddy could hook a new woman in his condition was a mystery to Mabel, but he did. Maybe he just wasn't very picky. One day Mabel had made her weekly call to see if he was okay and Sheila had answered the phone and that was that. She'd not heard anything from either of them until last night.

As a general rule, her father's women were at least pleasant to Mabel, some were even nice to her. One had been a school teacher who wanted to be a poet and had taught Mabel about meter and form and what was good and what was not so good in poetry. Another had been a pianist with a fondness for Ravel and Satie and took up teaching her where her mother had left off. Another had very carefully explained puberty to her—its joys and pitfalls—and Mabel figured that those lessons were at least half the reason why she'd never gotten knocked up. Another woman taught her how to type, which came in very handy over the years. A few were indifferent; only one downright hostile. She'd smacked Mabel for being breaking a plate and knocked her into the wall. Louie had been home and threw the bitch out in the street that very night. When the dust settled, her father had handed her a plate and told her to break it. Mabel had sailed it at the wall and knew this was as close to an apology she'd ever get from him. They played music until midnight when Mabel had to go to bed because she had school the next day.

So, Hackenbush and her father were not close, but they were allies. They'd had some fun together and after listening to people whine about their terrible parents, Hackenbush figured she could have drawn a worse hand.

She missed her mother and wished she knew where she

was. When Hackenbush moved to LA, she'd looked for her, but couldn't find a trace. Oh well, life goes on anyway, don't it?

The train pulled into the heavily tiled and stuccoed Santa Ana station and Hackenbush found a cab. She wished she could enjoy riding in a cab, but it was usually associated with not having a car (which was associated with being broke or nearly so) and therefore a big drag. "A drag on the finances, too," she thought as she paid the driver.

Standing in front of the nursing home, Hackenbush took a few deep breaths to steady her nerves. She didn't know what she'd find in there and wanted to be calm. She asked for her father at the reception desk and the nurse told her to go to the third floor and follow the noise.

It was eleven in the morning and the party in her father's room was in full swing. People were jammed in the hall and she could hear brass, saxophones and a banjo. Everybody who wasn't blowing a horn was singing *Sleepytime Down South*, one of her father's most favorite songs. Obviously, Sheila had gone through Louis' address book pretty thoroughly.

During a guitar solo, Hackenbush squeezed in and asked, "Is my Aunt Minnie in here?"

"Little Mabel is here! Little Mabel is here!" Aunt Dee Dee yelled. "Take the next chorus, honey." She wasn't a real aunt, but she'd known Mabel all Mabel's life and was a pretty good vibes player, too.

She danced a few steps to get closer to the hospital bed. Her father was propped up and wearing an oxygen mask. He was thinner, almost a skeleton, and pastier than the last time she'd seen him, but smiled at her with his eyes when she bent down to kiss him.

The impromptu band launched into *I've Got It Bad And That Ain't Good*, Hackenbush lending her voice to the others. Her father's friends were milling around, taking her aside to offer advice, help or just a hug. She'd known these people all her life, she called every one of them aunt or uncle and she'd even gigged with a few of them.

When she knew she was out of her father's sight, she

couldn't hold the tears back any longer. Her Uncle Norman told her to cool it.

"Only one could ever sing and cry at the same time was Judy Garland and not even she could do it too well," he said, giving her a shake. "Your daddy lived a happy life; let him die happy, Mabel. He could never stand to see you cry."

She said she'd try and they both laughed when *You, Rascal, You* started up. Louis Hackenbush was a rascal, but he was very much their rascal.

The management came by and said they'd call the police if there were more than five people at a time in the room, quietly in the room, from now on. They looked serious as a heart attack about the police, the kill-joys, so the party moved down to the lobby and people came up to visit in shifts.

Hackenbush shuttled between both places, catching up on gossip and being told, "My, how big you are now!" over and over. But it was okay; it was what these people always said. A few knew about the Lotus Room and asked her how she was getting along. Aunt Marie worked in a music store and told her to call her when she was ready to buy a new uke, she'd use her employee discount. Mabel said she would and hugged her.

Uncle Mike took her aside and handed her an envelope full of cash in small denominations. "We took up a little collection, Mabel," he said quietly. "You'll need it for later."

"Tell everybody I said thank you," she said, trying, unsuccessfully, not to cry.

A couple of hours later they were all gone and Mabel sat next to her sleeping father. "Not much of you left," she thought, looking at his flesh-less fingers. In spite of all the scotch, she'd slept very badly the previous night and nodded off. Patting on her hair woke her and she looked up at her father watching her over his oxygen mask. He gestured for her to come close and moved the mask so she could hear him.

"You're a good kid, Mabel, good singer, too," he hissed. "Sell my clarinet to bury me with." He coughed a deep, phlegmy cough and put the mask back on.

They sat silently together and in a little while he dozed off. He woke up a few times, looked confused and didn't know her. Hackenbush checked her watch and knew she'd have to make tracks to catch a train back to LA. He was breathing easily and peaceful, so she hoped he'd keep sleeping. He needed the rest...yeah, right.

She got up to go and found a dye-job redhead standing in the doorway.

"You Mabel?" Red asked.

"Yeah."

"I saw your picture," she said. "I'm Sheila."

"Oh...hi."

"Hi."

"Thanks for calling me and everybody," Hackenbush said, hoping she sounded more casual than she felt.

"You're welcome."

"He said to sell his clarinet to bury him with," she said, carefully avoiding the words "us" or "we." She watched Sheila nod slowly. "I have to catch a train..."

"Need a ride?"

"No...no, thanks," Hackenbush said, stepping past her. "I have it covered."

"See you then."

"Yeah, see you."

Thinking about her dad, she hardly noticed the train ride back to LA, but was exhausted when she got home. She put the envelope of cash under her mattress and went to sleep on top of it.

Sheila called at two to tell her that her father had died in his sleep and ask who she should call about selling the clarinet.

Hackenbush found out or rediscovered several things over the days following her father's death. She rediscovered how many friends she had since they all came out of the woodwork to condole her. This also reaffirmed how fast news traveled in her circle. She'd forgotten how many friends her father had since she'd not been around him much since she moved to LA. His friends were calling her and Sheila forwarded a sizeable stack of sympathy cards. She also found out that a used-up clarinet didn't fetch much on the modern market.

Aunt Marie did her best to find a buyer, but Louis had been sick for a long time and not playing his horn much, so it wasn't in great shape. And, probably because he was sick, he hadn't taken his usual meticulous care of it and it wasn't looking very good either. In the end Hackenbush took what Marie could get for it, added in the money Louis' friends put together and still came up way short for a burial. But not too short for a cremation.

This made her wince, mentally and physically. The Hackenbush clan, father and daughter, were not of a religious inclination. They had ironic Christmases for the girlfriends who required the tree and all the trimmings. As Christian holidays went, they thought it beat the hell out of Easter at least. For Louis and Mabel, Christmas was a busy time for casuals and a time to avoid shopping malls and that was about it. Otherwise, people were in better moods and often invited them over for really good food.

But the idea of cremation still made Mabel wince. There was too much weird history and stuff around it. Her own reaction was so strong; it could almost make her believe in tribal memory or something. She wasted an entire day pondering it. Paula very quietly took her aside and told her that "the firm and her friends" would make up the shortfall; no strings, no payback.

Mabel assumed this was Charles or Frank and Paula and probably Anna in there somewhere. And, who knew? Maybe some folks called Anna to contribute since Anna usually knew where Hackenbush was and what she was doing most of the time. Gigs, dates, voices from the past, and other ephemera had come via messages from Anna, so it was certainly possible.

But the only thing this generous offer did was snap her out of her funk. There's no such thing as no strings or no payback, maybe not in money, but certainly in karma or dues or whatever. And when people do you a favor, well, it just ups the potential to disappoint them farther down the road. It was never good to owe anyone too much or be at anybody's mercy, that was one of the important things she'd learned in life thus far. So, thanks, no thanks, she'd manage okay by herself as usual.

And, in truth, now that Hackenbush was de-funked and thinking on her feet again, she realized she just couldn't worry about something she didn't really believe in: if God couldn't figure out a body for her dead father on Judgment Day, then God must not be much of a God. And that summed it up for her. She still had to put some of her precious savings into paying for the cremation. Thank God Uncle Ray was willing to take charge of the ashes; he made a little alcove for them, with a picture of Louis in a tux no less, over the bar at his saloon. This would have pleased her father, she thought, sort of a continuous wake.

At any rate, once this was all settled, Hackenbush went down to close up Louis' apartment. For herself, she only took some photos and books, mostly music books. Louis' record collection had been sold a long time ago. Hackenbush had transferred as much of it to tape as she could, but she couldn't even find those in the mess. There wasn't much to deal with and none of it was worth anything, so she gave away what she could. A few neighbors took some of the furniture and kitchen stuff, but most of it went to St. Vincent de Paul Society. Hackenbush got her clothes and accessories from St. Vincent when she was hard up, so she had a soft spot for them. They got all the stuff she didn't have room for in her life.

Aunt Lo gave her a lift over to Uncle Ray's saloon and by the looks of it the party had shifted into high gear some time ago. Hackenbush, like everyone else there, had a lot to drink, sang very loudly and danced very well. Uncle John, who was permanently on the wagon, kept an eye on her and made sure she not only got to the station on time, but also got on the right train. It wasn't until she'd had a little nap between stops that Hackenbush realized Sheila was no longer around. She hadn't even noticed when the redhead slipped away. "I guess I should thank her...for something," Hackenbush thought. "If I ever see her again."

Paula leaned over their table at La Fonda and offered Hackenbush a job.

Hackenbush said thanks, no thanks.

"Why not?" Paula asked, offering her a cigarette and watching her tear the filter off before lighting it.

"I'm a singer not a secretary."

Paula hoped she hid her wince with a shrug. "It's a good job, Mabel."

"For somebody else," Hackenbush said. "Thanks though for extending this gig another week."

"I'm trying to extend it longer than that," Paula said. "Like permanently." She waved the waiter over and ordered another round of martinis.

"Permanent is one of those scary words for me, like 'should', 'normalcy', 'devolution', and 'Republican'," Hackenbush said, stubbing out her smoke.

"Hush!"

Hackenbush laughed, feeling almost mellow for the first time since her father died. "Sorry, Paula, didn't realize you were voting Republican these days."

"I'm not!"

"No? I thought it'd be required to go perm at Withers and Sons."

"Don't be an ass, Hackenbush," Paula snapped. "I'm still a liberal, I'm just a quiet one these days."

"I can dig it, Paula." Hackenbush sipped most of her martini. "Now, about Bobby–"

"What's it to ya, Hackenbush?"

"Oh, nothing." Mabel held up her hands in mock defense. "I just hate to see anyone who loves music enough to work as a busboy at the Storm Hill restaurant to be near it not pursue it, that's all."

"Don't be coy, Hackenbush." Paula downed her martini and waved the glass at the waiter to bring another round. "He has a crush on you."

"Nah; it's the way I sing and the band he's got a crush on."

"Nah."

"Yeah."

"Nah."

"Yeah."

"Yeah?"

"Yeah, Paula, you send that boy to music school and you'll see how fast he dumps me," Hackenbush said, chomping on her olive and glancing at their uneaten entrees.

"I guess," Paula said vaguely. "I've been saving and thinking he could, I don't know, get a business degree or something..."

"Practical?"

"Yeah."

"Well, fuck," Hackenbush said, collecting her gin-tinged thoughts. "Then don't send him to GIT."

"GIT?"

"Guitar Institute of Technology or the Grove School," she explained. "I hear Kenny Burrell is still at Fullerton; Bobby can major in music and minor in business."

"Or vice versa."

"Possible, but unlikely," Hackenbush said. "So he majors in music and minors in business and everybody is happy."

"Could work. Or maybe we should just leave the poor kid alone."

"So he rots in the mailroom? Right now he's digging it, but face it, Paula, how long can that last? He's smart, he's got good taste in music, he's cute–"

"He's not cute."

"I said cute, not desirable, just cute." Hackenbush laughed as Mama Tiger ordered another round and had their uneaten lunches cleared away. "He's got a lot going for him, it'd be a shame if he couldn't at least try to live his dream."

"Which is?" Paula asked, wondering why Hackenbush knew her kid so well. Was it just one musician to another, something Paula no longer was, or did Hackenbush just know something about life Paula had forgotten?

"I think it's a simple dream; he wants to be like Joey Bell or Gregg, have a band, play music and make people happy, that's all." Hackenbush sipped a little of her drink. "Besides, you know what Eric Liendsdorf said."

"Refresh my memory, please."

"Well, I can't remember the exact quote, but it was

basically that if you want to have a life in the arts, then try for it with all your might, because even if you fail and have to work in an office, at least you will have tried and will know more things because you have tried."

"You mean like the meaning of failure?"

"No, Paula, I mean like the exaltation of performing, even if it's only just once; you know something, you've felt something and you've risked for something more than just the next meal or rent check," Hackenbush said levelly. "That makes a person different and you can't un-know what you know from those experiences. So even if you fail, you haven't failed because you've succeeded in trying, you just haven't succeeded in succeeding, which is way overrated these days. Dig?"

"Dig," Paula said, glancing at her watch and deciding one two hour lunch in twelve years could be forgiven and if not, fuck 'em. "Success is overrated, Hackenbush? Since when?"

"Since it got confused with greed."

"Dig it."

They strolled through the Otis art gallery to sober up a little and then they walked down to look at the façade and foyer of the Elks Club to sober up some more. By the time they got back to the office, they were more or less clear-headed. Fortunately none of the partners were in that day, which explained why the music from the mailroom was a little louder than usual.

"What is that, Mabel?"

Hackenbush listened for a moment. "*Out There*; Dolphy on soprano sax and Ron Carter playing the 'cello."

"The 'cello, eh? Bobby's taste seems to be expanding. Is that your influence?"

"Well, sideways," she said. "He asked me where I learned to sing and I told him from listening to *Coltrane Sound*. Then he asked me about Eric Dolphy and I told him to listen to the stuff Dolphy did with Coltrane. The words *Out There* never left my mouth."

"Cool stuff," Paula said.

"No piano, no guitar; I can't imagine why Bobby likes

it. Seems like it would just annoy or distract him."

"Do you have this album?"

"I have two of this album."

"And?"

"And if I could gig without a piano or guitar, I'd do it, based on how cool this album is," Hackenbush said, listening to *17 West* go by. "But you can only push bar patrons so far."

"Ain't that the truth."

They strolled into the mailroom.

"Isn't this great!" Bobby shouted at them.

"I think I prefer Dolphy with a piano, don't you, Mabel?"

"Sometimes," Hackenbush said. "I thought you wanted some ideas on *My Favorite Things* or some other corny show tune like that?"

"This is cooler!"

"Is it?" Paula and Mabel asked in shocked voices. *My Favorite Things* was a song that defied most singers' efforts to make it cool. In fact, most singers never got anywhere near making it as cool had Coltrane had. And then you add in Dolphy...

"Yes; this is cooler, just take my word for it," Bobby said, puffing up a little.

"Well, Paula, I don't know about you, but I'm certainly not going to argue with the maestro here," Hackenbush said breathlessly.

"Not on this one, no," Paula said with a smile, thinking that Cal State Fullerton might really be the right place for him. "We shall leave you the field, Bobby, or the mailroom as the case might be."

And they did. A little while later, they heard him playing a live Coltrane and Dolphy concert version of *My Favorite Things*, so maybe he was listening to them after all.

"I hear you turned us down, Hackenbush," Charles asked over a Scotch a few evenings later. "Why is that? Paula was a little vague when I asked her."

"Don't like to hear the word 'no', do you, Charles?" Hackenbush asked, hoping to distract him.

"Yes, I don't. So why not work here? You have the skills, you can learn whatever you don't know, we'll pay for any courses you think you might need. Why not?"

Hackenbush mentally sighed and thought, "Because you'd try to own me, you'd want me to be dependant on the firm so I'd stay as long as you wanted me to stay, so you could rely on me, use me and shackle me here with a paycheck. Eventually, I'd get used to it, even need it and want it and forget that I was ever free and that I was never too much at anyone's mercy in so far as I could help it. And this is what is to be avoided at all costs, this is why I won't take your job, this is why I'd rather live on my own luck than your whim."

But she said, "I don't have the temperament for a perm job, Charles, I'd take it too seriously and if it didn't end in a few weeks, I'd burn out and get fired. Also, this job is wearing me out already; I go home and I'm too tired to sing. That's no life for me, sorry; let Anna find you someone who's ready to settle down—it's just not me, not now." She sipped her drink and started to open a fresh pack of Pall Malls. "Thanks for the sympathy flowers," she said. "How'd you know I like yellow roses?"

"I asked Bobby, he's our Hackenbush expert."

Hackenbush set the half opened pack on the desk. "Did he tell you the story behind it?"

"What story?"

"Well, he might not know," she said, resuming her getting-a-cigarette operations. "A couple of years ago there was this guy after me and I wasn't interested, but he kept bringing me roses. The first ones were dark red and I said that color was too sexual. So the next bundle was pink and I said they were too juvenile. The next were white and I said, 'What am I now? The Virgin Mary?'" She listened to Charles laugh. "See how it goes?" she continued. "So the next bundle was yellow and I said that was appropriate. And he said, 'Yeah, appropriate because all you do is piss on a guy,' and walked out. I never saw him again. Oh, go ahead and laugh, Charles; it's funny," she said, seeing him struggle. "And the larger truth is that I simply like yellow roses because they don't have much symbolic baggage for me."

"What about Texas?"

"As in *Yellow Rose Of*? Yeah, well, nice to know there's something good about it other than the jazz program at North Texas State," she said, tearing a match out of the book.

"Hey, don't light that!"

"Oh, sorry, I thought it was okay," she said, putting the match down.

"It is, I just have a present for you," he said, pushing a little foil-wrapped package across the desk. "Open it up."

"Wild, my initials on it and everything," she said, turning the gold Dunhill lighter over in her hand. "What's the occasion?"

"Nothing. I just saw it and thought if anyone should have it, it was you," he said, pouring more Scotch.

"Thank you, I'll think of you every time I light up now," she said, flicking her lighter open and adjusting the flame.

"Sorry about your father, Hackenbush," Charles said.

"Yeah," she said, exhaling a lung-full of smoke. "We weren't very close, but I'll miss him. I think he had a happy life; seemed like it anyway."

"Is your mother still living?"

"I've no idea, she left us when I was a kid."

"Sorry."

"About what?"

"I don't mean to pry."

"You're not."

"Or cause you anymore pain."

"Pain?" she asked and then shrugged. "It's more like sorrow. Pain is when you struggle against sorrow; there's nothing to struggle with in this situation. My dad got lung cancer and died; my mom decided to find a better life somewhere else and left—there's nothing I could do for or about either of them. I loved them, I miss them and life goes on."

"That's a good attitude to have about it."

"It'll do. Anything else just slows me down," she said, stubbing out her cigarette and looking at her watch. "No politics tonight, Charles?"

"No," he said, shaking his head. "Not tonight."

"Anything you especially want to hear on Saturday?" she asked.

"I'd like to hear some of the songs you sang in the Island Room," he said. "Although you were very good in both places, I liked those songs better than the ones at the Oak Room."

"Thanks," she said, getting up. "I'll see you later."

"I won't be in the rest of the week, I've got court dates and meetings," he said, also rising. "I'll miss you around the office, Hackenbush."

"I'll miss you, too, Charles," she said, extending her hand over his desk. "But we'll both get over it."

They shook and she left. While waiting for her cab in the lobby, she asked the security guard on duty to tell Walter that Hackenbush said "Hi". He said he would and she thanked him. Her taxi pulled up under the street lamp and she got in and went home.

That Friday afternoon, Paula signed Hackenbush's last timecard and checked the "Assignment completed" box. "Call me if you change your mind about the job, Mabel," she said, tearing off her copy of the form.

"I shall," Hackenbush said, knowing she never would.

"I talked to Bobby about Fullerton last night," Paula said a little too casually. "Played him a Kenny Burrell album."

"What did he say?"

"He said he'd think about it."

"A thoughtful type of cat, your Bobby."

"Isn't he just?"

Hackenbush hadn't exactly been avoiding Frank, nor was he avoiding her; they were just making a point of not making eye contact since she'd hauled him out of that mid-town den of iniquity. He had thanked her in a hurried, furtive way and Belinda had called her to say how grateful they both were to her. And all that was great as long as they kept their problems away from her—it was not a request, it was a requirement.

Anyway, on her last day at Withers and Sons,

Hackenbush went up to the roof to smoke a cigarette and take her last look at the view. She would miss that roof, she would miss Bobby and Paula and the redheaded punk and Adela, who'd given her a decoupage creation of a top-hatted Duke Ellington—something Hackenbush was reasonably sure no other singer in town had—as a good-bye present. Nice kid, Adela, and Hackenbush hoped she'd find some nice lady someday to make decoupage things for.

And speaking of nice kids, Alan had taken her for a farewell lunch at the Royale and given her a tin soldier, brightly painted and standing at attention, to remember him by. She'd said that it was certain she'd never forget him and would put her soldier in a safe place, which would be in a box in her closet with her decoupage Duke, but she didn't mention that.

So she was thinking of all this as she strolled along the parapet when the roof door banged open and Frank joined her. Well, that was okay, she was on her second cigarette and she'd only come up to smoke one so it was probably time to leave anyway.

"I guess I'll see you tomorrow night," he said abruptly.

"Unless you toss me off the roof now," she thought, but merely nodded and crushed out her cigarette. "Well, good-bye, Frank, it's been swell knowing you," she said, sticking out her hand, which he ignored.

"He told Belinda about the lighter."

"So?"

"He bought it while he was buying her a diamond necklace."

"So?"

Frank had no answer for this and just looked really uncomfortable.

"So, I have a nice lighter and Belinda has a diamond necklace and no guts," Hackenbush said matter-of-factly. "Face it, Frank, you love a nice girl who is too afraid of pissing people off to run away and marry you. Find somebody else; it's a big town, lots of women. How about some gorgeous knock-out of a failed starlet? Lots of those in town - devastatingly beautiful with not quite enough of whatever that

127

something is that makes one babe an A-list starlet and another babe just a rich guy's wife. Go get one of those and live it up while you can."

"Look, Hackenbush, if it's a matter of money..." Frank began after a few moments.

"No sale, buddy."

"Money just doesn't impress you, does it?"

"Only its lack, Frank, only its lack," she said, heading for the elevator.

"You've never been in love, Hackenbush," Frank said bitterly to her back.

"Oh, yes I have," she said, over her shoulder. "But as you can see, I survived it."

Meanwhile downtown, not too far from Hackenbush's aerie, Eddy Lee was changing his Greyhound bus for the RTD and heading up to Pasadena to look up his old pal Cody Cole.

A few hours later, Shorty got out of bed to answer the phone and nearly dropped it.

"Hey, Shorty, Mabel still live in the same place?" Eddy asked with his usual cool.

"Aughga..."

"Look, Shorty, I know this is kinda a surprise..."

"Ahowa..."

"Way I left and been gone, but now I'm back, ya know how it is—you can never really leave LA for good—and, um, Cody tells me there's nobody new in her life, but, ah, that you probably know what's going on under her wig best, like, dig?" Silence. "Shorty?"

"Um, Eddy, I dunno," Shorty sighed at last. "She says she's over you but, well, she still has that picture of you two by her bed."

"That's a good sign," Eddy said.

"For you," Shorty said, regretting he'd mentioned it.

"I wanna see her."

"Get her number from somebody else," Shorty said. "And leave me out of it." He hung up and went back to bed. His new lover rolled over and sleepily asked him who called. "Eddy Lee is back in town."

"Oh my God! Does he want his job back?" Gregg asked, sitting up in alarm.

"Not exactly."

"Eddy called me," Ross said as they were packing up.

"Eddy Lee?" Hackenbush asked. They'd just finished a casual in Encino that Friday night.

"Yup. He's back in town. Wants to see you."

"Did you tell him to come down to the Lotus Room, Thursday through Sunday, by the grace of the wonderful Mr. Tanaka, nine PM to one AM, downtown LA time?"

"Nah, but that's not a bad idea," Ross said, gathering up his sticks and brushes.

"What did you tell him?" she asked while tidily winding up her microphone cord.

"I got his number and told him you'd call him if you felt like it," Ross said, handing her a scrap of paper.

"This is Cody's number," she said, crumpling it up.

"That's where he's camped for now."

"Fuck." She looked into Ross' wry, sympathetic face. "Well, fuck, I guess we do know a lot of the same people, but I wish he'd stay away from my band."

"Our band, and we were his band before he brought you in, Mabel, don't forget," Ross said.

"How could I ever forget when I have you to remind me?" she asked coolly. "Hope he doesn't want his old job back."

"Which one?"

"All of them."

On Saturday afternoon, Aunt Marie drove up with Hackenbush's new baritone ukulele. Unfortunately, she'd caught traffic and Hackenbush just had time to write her a check, give her a cold drink and a peck on the cheek before she had to run out the door with Cody to go do Charles's engagement party.

"You stay out of trouble, little Mabel," Marie warned.

"I will, Auntie. Sorry I can't go out and play tonight," Hackenbush said, stowing the uke, still in its box, by the piano.

"You're missing a good time, doll, Vince Young is playing at a place called the Island Room tonight," Marie said. "I'm having dinner with Jane and Phil Davis and then we're going. Too bad you can't join us."

"Really is too bad," Hackenbush said and meant it. "Sorry I'll miss Uncle Vince and Aunt Jane and Uncle Phil, but try to have dinner at the Island Room, the food is to die for."

"I'll mention it, sweetie. Sing your heart out tonight," Marie said, waving good-bye.

"It's just a casual, Aunt Marie."

"Don't matter what you're doing, Mabel, but how you do it, never forget that."

"Yes, ma'am," Hackenbush said, waving as Cody pulled away and headed West.

"So, what's with Eddy Lee, Cody?" she asked when they were safely away.

He gave her the basic run-down: Eddy was back in LA, looking for work and a place, and wanted to see her.

"Why?"

Cody thought Eddy still loved her and realized he'd made a mistake leaving her.

"It took him four years to figure that out?"

Obviously. "So, what do you think, Mabel?"

"I dunno what to think," she said, lighting a cigarette in aid of cognition. "He leaves and he comes back and wants to see me. If I was him, I'd be afraid to see me."

"Why's zat?"

"The way he left: no warning, just a message on my fucking machine that he's not the right guy and it's not the right time," she said, tapping some ash out the window. "What kind of asshole..."

"Well, at least he didn't say you're not the right girl at the right time," Cody offered helpfully.

"Comes down to the same thing, pal. He. Left. Me." Hackenbush stared out the window at Wilshire. She didn't turn her head as they passed the Withers and Sons building.

"He still wants to see you, Mabel," Cody said. "What are you going to do?"

"Aside from the best I can, I've no idea," she said, tossing her cigarette into the gutter. "Where is he? He better not show up at this thing."

"Calm down," Cody growled. "He rustled up a car today and he's out sitting in and making himself known again in LA."

"Well, I guess the town could use another good guitar player," she said, adjusting her spandex skirt.

"Gregg called me, he's a little nervous that you'll give Eddy his old job back."

"Which one?" she thought, but said, "Tell him to relax, he's less of a pain– I mean, he's easier to work with than Eddy ever was. He's got the gig until he pisses me off or he quits. Simple. Dig?"

"Dig."

Suzy really knew how to throw a party when she was spending other people's money. There was a huge marquee on the patio, an eight course sit-down dinner inside and oceans of excellent booze.

For Hackenbush, the best part was the decent PA system, band stand and a nice dinner for all of them. Oh, and the money was pretty good, too.

On the way in, Hackenbush had exchanged waved and nods with most of the valet parking staff. She saw one of them wave Shorty past the parking area so he could park his moped by the kitchen door and thought that was damn nice of them. Looking around at the catering staff, she realized that Suzy had hired party-throwing-type firms that hired all the cash-strapped-type artists in town. Suzy only laughed when Hackenbush mentioned this over the tasteful Sinatra record playing in the background.

"Of course; how else would it be?" she asked.

"Who'd you hire for security?" Hackenbush asked, watching what could only be, to her trained eye, a bouncer, factor or all-purpose frightener.

"Not mine, Hackenbush," Suzy said, looking wary.

"Those are Withers Senior's security guys."

"Why the hell...?"

"Not that anyone would remember, but he ran for public office about ten years ago," Suzy said quietly. "He lost, of course, but he got some hate mail and has had his own security squad ever since. Makes him feel safe."

"Are they as scary as they look?" Hackenbush asked, watching one of them moving through the crowd.

"Kind of; they're cold as ice," Suzy said, after a moment's thought. "They might make Withers Senior feel safe, but they make me nervous."

"How so?" Hackenbush asked, wondering what she'd gotten poor Suzy into.

"They're like guards guarding him from something," Suzy said.

"Like the big bad city of LA?" Ross asked in his big bad drummer voice.

"Or the heathens to the south and east?" Cody asked melodramatically.

"Or the hairdressers of West Hollywood?" Shorty lisped at her.

"Or all those low-life musicians like us?" Gregg asked, pushing his empty plate aside.

"Hmmm, well, if so, we've flown in under the radar, Hackenbush," Ross rumbled.

This all made Suzy laugh and lighten up, which was the whole point, really.

"Or maybe," Hackenbush chimed in at last. "Maybe those guards aren't protecting him from the city and its denizens. Maybe they're protecting the city and its denizens from him."

They roared; even the catering staff laughed discreetly.

"Hey, Bobby!" Hackenbush called. "What are you doing in that outfit?"

"If I work for the caterers, I'm close enough to hear you sing," he said, returning her firm handshake.

"I'm surprised you weren't invited to this thing," Hackenbush said, shielding him from his boss' gaze.

"Only the older employees are; mom, Adela and the staff

attorneys are here," he said smiling and then grew serious. "Hackenbush, I–"

"There you are, Hackenbush!" Withers Senior rolled himself up to her side. "And Bobby, too; rather strangely dressed for a party."

"I'm working for the caterers tonight, Mr. Withers," Bobby told him.

"Excellent, shows initiative to take extra jobs," Withers snarled. "Keep them in line for us tonight, young man."

"Yes, sir," Bobby said, hearing it for the dismissal it was. He gave Hackenbush's spandex-clad arm a pat and went away.

"Nice dress, Hackenbush," Withers Senior said.

"Tight enough for you, Mr. Withers?" she asked blandly.

"Yes, quite revealing," he said slowly. "Who'd have known you had all that under those baggy dresses you wore around the office."

"That's exactly the point of those baggy dresses," she said coolly. "That and fluorescent lights, nobody looks good under them."

"Quite. Well, we'll look forward to your performance," he said, waving Suzy over. "Everyone says you can sing. I suppose I'll find out. Let's go, Suzy."

Hackenbush noted that he'd already dropped the please and thank yous for Suzy and wondered again what kind of a mess she'd gotten the poor dancer into.

"What a fucking jerk," Gregg said under his breath.

"God, no wonder he didn't get elected," Ross said quietly.

"We're out of here in three hours, guys, and two bills richer, relax, have another drink," Hackenbush said, refusing to allow Withers et al to bother her. "Oh, there's Carlos," she said, waving the conga player over.

"Diva baby!"

"Have some dinner, Carlos," she said, getting a whiff of him and a vicarious high. "And I hope you saved some for us for after the job."

"Always, my diva, always."

As much as Hackenbush told herself she wouldn't let Withers et al bother her, they, and a few other things, were bothering the hell out of her.

Was she the only one who thought Frank and Belinda looked miserable? That Charles looked stunned? That Belinda's parents looked like overdressed junkies? And that, aside from a few familiar faces, didn't this crowd look like it might kill and eat its weaker members just to let off a little steam?

Okay, so the crowd was fairly normal for this kind of scene. Still, that coupled with the happy/unhappy couple was giving her the creeps.

After their first break, she asked the band to play some sambas while she got some air in the garden. The marquee installers had thoughtfully provided outdoor heaters in case the night got chilly, but all they were doing for Hackenbush were making the air hot and heavy.

It was a nice evening, not cold, but just cool enough to make pacing and heat-retaining spandex comfortable. And smoking; smoking was always more pleasant for Hackenbush in cool weather.

When her head cleared, she realized that Eddy's reappearance was bothering her, too. He wanted to see her; okay, fine, she'd see him and get it over with. What was the worst that could happen? She'd find out she was still in love with him? He was still in love with her? Or no one was in love anymore? Or some horrible combination of the above? That would be bad, but survivable because, in truth, almost everything is survivable, whether you want it to be or not.

She exhaled a huge lungful of smoke and blew her Eddy-ing thoughts away with it. She'd wandered into a little stone-paved clearing and found a discreet place to stub out her cigarette and listen to the band play *Triste*. She liked this wistful tune, it reminded her of wanting something she could not have, but only feeling sorrow about it, not rage or fear or...

"Hello, Hackenbush. Getting some air?"

"Hello, Charles. Yes, I needed to get out of those lights," she said.

"Are you having a good time?" he said after a few beats

of silence.

"I'm working, Charles; but, yeah, I'm having a good time. Are you?"

"Of course," he said a little too quickly and then asked her if she'd like to dance.

"Sure."

They danced; he held her close, it's the only way to dance a samba, really. Hackenbush thought he danced fairly well, a little stiffly, but what can you do?

"Does this song have words?" he asked.

"It does."

"Will you sing them for me?"

"Yeah, wait, it's almost at the top again..." The words were sad, but not tragic, and they made her mellow enough to let down her guard a little.

Probably she had too much on her mind and he was very handsome, here in the dark, and it just seemed right to let him lean her back and kiss her. And perhaps they felt more for each other than they wanted to admit, but the difference between them was telling. Whereas Hackenbush, because Charles was in fact about to marry someone else, would have simply walked away from this pleasant kiss, Charles, on the other hand, decided to be a jerk about it.

Bending her farther back, he broke the kiss and murmured her name. Then he dropped her on the pavement and said, "Hackenbush, you're fired," and walked back to his party, his life and his place in the dominant social group.

"You son of a bitch," she said, looking up at the trees and clouds above her. "I don't even work for you." And then she was looking at Shorty leaning over her.

"I hope he's a better kisser than dancer," he said, helping her up.

"He is a son of a bitch."

They turned when the band played a fanfare and some male started to talk.

Hackenbush squared her shoulders and got a determined look in her eyes.

"Whatcha gonna do, Hackenbush?" he asked, nervously eyeing what he thought of as her fighting posture.

"The worst I can," she said, striding toward the bandstand where Belinda's father was about to congratulate the happy couple.

He never got to; or at least not that anyone heard because Hackenbush yanked the mike out of the PA system.

"*Goodbye look*" she snarled at Carlos, who launched into the conga part and took the rest of the band with him.

Hackenbush could really shake it when she was so inclined. She combined a wide, slow shimmy with a fiery Flamenco stomp and the pure violence of simulated fucking. It was amusing and innocent-seeming to onlookers, but it was aimed directly at Charles and all he could do was go where she herded him. Swinging the unplugged mike cord like a lasso, Hackenbush danced forward and very deftly separated Charles from his little group. She noticed Frank whispering to Belinda as he pulled her out of lashing range. She sang the chorus unaided by amplification in her best bel canto voice so that it carried over the crowd and, more importantly, battered Charles, the cad. Using the dead mike cord like a whip, she drove him along the edges of the dance floor. She closed the distance between them, shoved him into a chair and tipped it precariously back.

Menacingly, she leaned over him and said, "You can't fire me, I'm a temp." She leaned a little closer. "And that assignment ended yesterday," she added, letting the chair fall back.

Charles took a moment to recover from his bump before he bellowed for security.

One of the guards made the mistake of grabbing Hackenbush, who'd already lost interest in the subject, by her hair and hauling her away from Charles.

Seeing this, something snapped in Suzy and she rammed the first thing she could find into the guard. That thing happened to be Withers Senior in his wheelchair, but it had the same effect: the goon let go of Hackenbush.

Two other security personnel came rushing out of their cages when Withers Senior started to howl. A member of the catering staff accidentally pushed a cart of food into one's path. And the other guard mysteriously tripped as he passed

Shorty and fell into a table of Charles's drunken former Fraternity brothers, who were, as you can well imagine, not amused.

In the general melee that followed, Suzy shut off the lights and Hackenbush found the sound system and cranked up the Sinatra record to deafening levels. While she inside, she was looking for her coat and shoulder bag, mainly so she could put her mike in it and split, but she found the most considerate Shorty Smith gathering them up for her. "Get your moped and get outta here, darlin'," she gasped at him, shoving her mike in the bag on her shoulder.

"It's by the kitchen," he said. "I can—"

"See you later, baby." She blew him a kiss and was out the door.

Dashing around the edges of the brawl, Hackenbush saw the band was packed and leaving the stand. Two of the valet parking guys were standing by with the cart they'd used to haul the stuff into the back yard and three other valet guys had Ross's van, Cody's wagon, and Carlos' battered sedan lined up, revved up and ready for flight. Better than any precision drill team, they loaded and were away. She saw Suzy jump into Carlos' car and he sped off. She further noticed Frank and Belinda in his BMW speeding off as well. Not having time to properly reflect on that, she filed it away for later.

Still trying to get around the confusion on the patio, Hackenbush ran back into the garden. This would swing her in a wide arc away from the brawl in progress, but would take longer to get to the sanctuary of the parking area. She'd caught sight of Charles, upright again, in the crowd and didn't like the look on his face. The bad part was that he saw her, too. Running down the garden path as fast as her heels and skirt would allow, she glanced over her shoulder and saw Charles gaining on her. "Well, hopefully he won't break too many of my bones," she thought, hearing him overtaking her. Very much suspecting it was in vain, she put on a sprint, fully expecting him to grab her by the hair and jerk her off her feet. This did not happen; instead she heard a small engine, a thump and a crash in the bushes. And then Shorty was next to her on his moped. She caught a glimpse of Charles sprawled in the shrubbery, trying to get up again. In her tight skirt, she hopped sidesaddle onto the back of Shorty's chariot. "I thought you split," she yelled in his ear.

"I saw Charles see you before you saw him," he yelled back. "I thought you might need a ride, sister."

"'Deed I did," she agreed, and was silent as he sped her out of the garden and into the parking area where Cody and his van were waiting. A couple of valet guys heaved Shorty's moped in beside Cody's bass and Shorty wedged himself in between the two to keep them apart.

"My heroes!" she yelled from the van window as Cody pulled away from the riot. Good thing, too, because the sirens were getting closer. But that would be someone else's problem because she and the band were gone by then.

Since they were in that part of town anyway, the three of them went to Pipers to recover and she filled Cody in on the scene in the garden.

"I wasn't the only one watching in the bushes," Shorty said, when she was finished. "That Frank guy was there, I saw Bobby there, and I think I caught a glimpse of Paula and Suzy."

"Don't people have better things to do than spy on me at parties?" she asked, salting her eggs.

"Sounds like it was worth spying on, Mabel," Cody said. "What got into you? Or didn't get into you, maybe?"

"Ha ha, Cody, how amusing," she growled. "Y'know, a guy like Charles, he's used to having everything his own way. It was a nice kiss and then he had to go and ruin it by being a jerk. Well, there are just some things he can't be a jerk about and I can be a jerk, too."

"A first-class jerk, too," Cody said.

"So, it was a kind of jerk-off for you and this Charles guy?" Shorty asked.

Hackenbush sat back to think about this for a moment. "Yeah, and now I feel so much better," she said, lighting a cigarette with her gold monogrammed lighter. "So, so much better."

"And Frank and Belinda had nothing to do with it?" Shorty asked after letting her smoke in peace for a while.

"Who are they?" Cody asked.

She had a few more moments of peace while Shorty filled Cody in on the doomed romance. "No, I was and am pissed off at Charles, the jerk, but if I bought those two another night to grow some courage, then I suppose that's good," she said wearily. "And if this gives her the guts or whatever to dump Charles, that will be a bonus thing he can't have his way."

"Man, you sure don't like that Charles guy, do you, Mabel?" Cody asked.

"Dunno," she said mysteriously from her cloud of smoke. "Maybe I liked him more than I knew I did."

Paula tried her best not to work on Sundays, but that Sunday morning was different; she was going in to draft her resignation letter and hoped it wouldn't take too long.

The scene last night had been the last straw. She'd not wanted to stumble upon Withers Junior and Hackenbush, but there they were and it was like a car accident one just couldn't look away from; a very graceful car accident, but a wreck nonetheless.

Paula had been annoyed when Withers Junior started putting the moves on Hackenbush, but knew the singer could take care of herself. And a very few minutes after he kissed her, Hackenbush had proved that. Squared.

What bothered Paula was the Withers clan's assumption that everyone in their orbit was there to serve them. As far as Paula could see there was nothing good natured or comradely in the Withers-Hackenbush kiss or in their whole interaction so far. Hackenbush might have been amusing herself with the flirtation, but Withers Junior was trying to dominate her and then dismiss her. That was his usual procedure and why he went through so many intelligent, competent secretaries. If one had any will or mind of her own, Withers Junior crushed it at the first opportunity. And Withers Senior was worse; who did Withers Junior learn it from anyway?

However, whatever Withers Junior was trying to prove by dominating and dismissing Hackenbush had backfired badly on him. Suzy's quick thinking had probably saved

Hackenbush from being hurt by the hired maulers; it had definitely started the brawl of the season. In the ensuing chaos, Paula had slipped away to think it over.

What bothered her most was that she could no longer excuse the Withers for being bastards just because they paid her. She worked hard and they paid her fairly, but it was no longer enough. Hackenbush had opened an old wound in Paula by reminding her that she had been a singer once and a good one, and was still a singer, a good one. It hurt because it reminded her what living was, and what living she wasn't doing and hadn't been doing for too many years. But Hackenbush, probably unconsciously and unwillingly because she didn't want the competition, had opened the door of Paula's cell and Paula, who'd tried to resist it, was ready to be free again.

Paula's biggest reason for staying in a job she now hated had been shown to be hollow. Again, Hackenbush's mere presence in the office had proved to her that Bobby was old enough to mostly take care of himself. And he was a resourceful kid; in the days since he'd decided to go to Cal State Fullerton, he'd dug up what little money there was out there for working class college students.

They would both temp or get part time jobs. Adela, too, since she was as horrified that Withers Junior would wimp out and sic his father's huge security guards on Hackenbush, who, in Adela's opinion, wasn't doing anything life-threatening. A bully is the most disgusting thing in the world, she had said, and Paula had quietly agreed. So, Paula had let the answering machine pick up at midnight and take a message from Adela, calling from Kinkos in Glendale, that she'd fax in her notice and wanted it to be effective that very night since it was only eleven forty-five PM and would shave two days off what she'd have to work at Withers and Sons.

The smell of coffee in the office tipped Paula off that someone, hopefully not Withers Junior, was in there. Alas, it was he; unshaven, rumpled and wearing the same evening clothes he'd had on last night.

"Morning," she said, taking Adela's letter off the fax machine. "What brings you in on a Sunday, Mr. Withers?"

"There's more Scotch here than at home," he said, running his hand over his stubble. "Or at least there was."

"Ah." Paula eased past him and first went into the mailroom and turned on the copier. While it was warming up, she went into her office and she quickly typed up a letter giving a month's notice. She took it, Bobby's scribbled note and Adela's neatly typed faxed letter into the mailroom, made three copies, put one copy in each of their mailboxes, the other two copies into her purse, shut down the copier and turned off the lights. She did this carefully and methodically, all the while screwing up her courage to hand in the resignations to Withers Junior Or perhaps she'd do it on Monday, when there were more people around; she didn't like the look of him much just then. She dug out the florist's bill for Hackenbush's sympathy flowers to get the singer's home address so she could pay her a call that afternoon. She wanted to tell her in person what she was doing and thank her sincerely. Also, perhaps to warn her that she would have some competition in the near future. She turned off her computer and was jotting Hackenbush's home address down when Withers Junior buzzed her to come into his office. "Yes, sir?" she asked, standing in the doorway holding her coat and the three letters of resignation.

"I suppose you saw that...that episode last night," he said, sounding as bitter as he looked. "Can you possibly explain that lunatic's behavior?"

"If you mean the security guard that attacked Hackenbush, I suppose he did that because your father pays him to do that kind of thing," Paula said slowly so her anger wouldn't make her trip over her words. "If you mean Suzy, she was defending a woman being attacked by a much larger man." She swallowed and took a deep breath. "And if you mean Hackenbush, I imagine she doesn't like being kissed and dumped on the pavement like a used...used something anymore than any other sane woman does."

Withers Junior came around his desk and loomed over Paula in a way that usually cowed her. The glint in her eye made him take a step back. What he couldn't know was that in Paula's past she had faced down club owners, panhandlers,

141

teenaged boys, conductors, school principals, bill collectors, gigolos and recently even Hackenbush at the Island Room, and compared to all that, Charles Withers Junior was a punk and a piker. "So you saw all that in the garden," he said, trying to sound nonchalant. "I'm sure you misunderstood."

"I doubt it, Mr. Withers, I wasn't born yesterday and neither was Hackenbush. Here," she said extending the letters.

"What's this?"

"We quit; me, Bobby and Adela just quit."

"You're fired then."

"You can't fire us; we just quit," she said, turning away. "But if we are fired, we'll be in on Monday to pick up our stuff. Good-bye, Mr. Withers."

Charles stood there, envelopes in hand, mouth open until he could speak again. "Paula..." But he heard the elevator doors close and knew she was gone. He dropped the letters on his desk, thinking of ways he could get them to stay: more money, more paid vacation time, more...something. He paced the hall, remembering the look in Paula's eyes; defiant, cocksure and amused behind a certain wariness. Same look as he'd enjoyed seeing on Hackenbush all this time, all those nights over all that scotch. And then when he held her close and she sang those sad words to him, he just had to be a jerk to her because he could. Or he'd thought he could, now he wasn't so sure. His chest felt tight and he felt bad; he wanted her back in any way he could get her back. He found himself staring into Paula's dim office and noticed a paper on her usually immaculate desk. Anything to take his mind off Hackenbush. He shrugged and turned on the lights.

It was the florist bill with Hackenbush's home address on it.

Hackenbush spent the morning putting ice on her shoulders, which the hired mauler had wrenched when he grabbed her last night, and playing her new baritone ukulele. She'd play the uke until she hurt too much and then get out the ice pack and read a few pages of *Farewell My Lovely*. She liked *The Long Goodbye* better, especially since the book made much more sense than any of the films of it. But Chandler was dead, and probably wouldn't have cared anyway.

She was a little anxious. Cody had called earlier and asked if he and Eddy could come by for a few minutes. She said, yes, and wished they get there so she could get it over with. To distract herself she picked up the baritone, which was fast becoming a pal, and played through *I Had a Notion* a few times. There are lots of songs about men not showing up where they said that they would be one morning, noon or night, but *I Had a Notion* was a particularly good one.

"No, you didn't show up, did you, Eddy? But you did leave a message," she said out loud, putting the ice pack back on. "A message on my machine to tell me we were through." So she had some apprehension to go with her pain while she rested. Enough of that; she stood up and launched into the more rousing *Me, Myself and I,* dancing with the new uke, acclimating herself to its weight and balance. The song was going quite well when the bell rang. But it was Suzy, not Eddy.

"Hackenbush!"

"La Suzy!" Hackenbush waved her to a chair. "Thanks for the rescue last night; I guess you're out of a job now?"

"Yeah, well, fuck that," Suzy said. "I was sick of those guys anyway. Here," she extended a stack of envelopes. "I made sure to get the cash to pay the band on Friday; hope you don't mind handing it out."

"Not at all, darling; you're my hero," Hackenbush said, shoving the money into her purse. "Carlos will be pleased, he left a message last night whining that we'd never get paid."

"If it was up to anybody else this morning, you wouldn't," Suzy laughed.

"Maybe you had a premonition?"

"Or maybe I just know how slow caterers are to pay sometimes," she said. "And I know you need the money, Hackenbush."

"'Deed I do, I pick up the car tomorrow." She offered Suzy some coffee. "Roberto the wonderful kept it an additional week and didn't charge me storage. Still a grand for the tranny, though."

"Ah, money," Suzy said vaguely and then looked her in the eye. "Hackenbush, what the hell were you doing last night?"

"Proving that even though I don't have money or belong to the dominant social group, I still have very effective ways to defend myself," she said.

"I guess," Suzy said over her coffee cup. "Charles Withers, Junior sure can't take a joke, can he?"

"No, and– dammit." Hackenbush frowned at the door. "Suzy, d'you mind waiting in the bedroom for a few minutes? This won't take long." She waved her though the doorway by the piano and closed the door.

"You?" Hackenbush stepped back to let Shorty and Gregg in. "It's a little late for brunch isn't it?"

"Hackenbush, am I fired or what?" Gregg demanded. Shorty only rolled his eyes at her.

"Or what; unless you did something weird I don't know about yet," she said.

"No! But everybody knows Eddy Lee is back."

"So?"

"So! He sat in at the Island Room last night and was a smash hit," Gregg said, starting to pace. "Some old woman tried to beat him up, but aside from that it was a great night."

Hackenbush gently blessed Aunt Marie for her loyalty and winked at Shorty. "Look, Gregg, I won't say Eddy isn't a great guitar player because he is, but he's a prima donna pain in the ass, too. And so are you, but you didn't break my fucking heart four years ago, so I'll keep you until one of us, you or me, gets sick of it, okay?" She swung round at the doorbell. "Oh, fuck! D'you mind hanging out in my bedroom for a few minutes?" she asked, digging in her purse for Shorty's and Gregg's envelopes and handing them over as she herded them into the adjacent room. Thoughtful Suzy had written all their names on them in her lovely round hand.

"What the...?"

"He's all upset, Hackenbush, calm him down," Ross said in that exasperated Ross voice he did so well.

"We will never get paid, diva, because of your insane, but charming, dancing last night," Carlos wailed at her. He looked like he hadn't slept and smelled like he'd been drinking all night.

"Ross?" she asked, turning to her drummer.

"He showed up at my place this morning," Ross said patiently. "I fed him, I coffeed him, I did all that I could do for him. I wouldn't let him drive here, though."

"Probably a good thing," Hackenbush said, digging out their envelopes. "I thought you had a church gig, Ross?"

"The youth choir is touring this week, so I'm off the hook," Ross said, thumbing quickly through his cash. "Jesus loves us, Hackenbush."

"As manifested by his favorite ballet dancing babe, La Suzy. I'll tell you later," she said, trying to pry off Carlos, who had fallen on his knees and clasped her legs. "Um, Ross, if you would be so kind...?"

"C'mon, guy, let's take the money and run," Ross said, pulling Carlos up. "You oughta dance like that a little more often, Hackenbush, could be good tips."

"Wang would never allow it," she said and then cursed at the door again and asked them to step in to her bedroom.

Expecting Eddy Lee, it turned out to be Paula. "I just quit my job or got fired," she said. "Either is fine."

"What?"

"I can't work for those people anymore! No one can make me do it!"

"No one is going to," Hackenbush said, glancing out the window at the parking situation; it was getting crowded on her little street. "What are you going to do?"

"Start singing again," Paula said flatly.

"Ooooh...how niiiiice..." Hackenbush almost wailed, but kept her smile frozen on her face.

"Look, Hackenbush, you've got the Lotus Room and gigs with guys like Carlos," Paula said reasonably. "I'll take the guys like Lowell and joints on the west side. We'll divvy up the town; neither of us can take all the gigs, can we?"

"Are you always this sensible, Paula?" Hackenbush asked after thinking it over for a few moments.

"I'm thinking very clearly this morning." Paula smiled. "Now, about last night...?" She looked a question at Mabel when a masterful knock sounded on the door.

"A girl can try to have a quiet Sunday and fail," Hackenbush said. She ushered Paula into her bedroom and promised to liberate them all very soon.

"Hackenbush! What the fuck!? I've had a dozen calls about what you did last night." Anna stomped in.

"Wouldn't it have been easier to phone, Anna?"

"I was having brunch in Pasadena with Lola Rae, she was working the catering gig last night," Anna said.

"Oh yes, we waved at each other."

"She said you're a madwoman, but a good 'un. And Suzy, too!" Anna took a deep breath. "Hackenbush, Withers and Sons hasn't paid me for the last week you were there yet, what am I–" The doorbell cut her off mid-worry.

"Well, why not discuss it with Paula and Suzy in my bedroom?" She ushered the shocked sole proprietor into it and went to see who was at the door.

"Bobby? What's up?"

"I came to see if you're all right, doc," he said, shyly stepping into the room.

"How'd you get my address?"

"Off the florist bill in the office," Bobby said, looking around her lair. "Are you okay, Hackenbush? That guy grabbed you pretty hard."

"My shoulders are a little fucked up, but I'm on aspirin and ice, so I'll be okay by tomorrow." She smiled at the thoughtful little guy.

He looked down and then up, into her eyes. "Hackenbush, I..." He jumped when the doorbell rang.

"I hate to do this to ya, kid," she said, sending him into the same room with his mother, who would probably want to know what the hell he was doing visiting a dangerous character like Hackenbush on a Sunday.

"Finally," she sighed at Eddy and Cody.

"What the...?" Cody asked.

"Hi, Mabel," Eddy said, looking her over. "Nice place. How you been?"

"Fine, Ed. You?" she asked, digging Cody's money envelope out of her purse. "We got lucky and by the grace of

La Suzy," she said, handing it to him and telling him the story.

"Two hundred for a casual that you started a fight at?" Eddy asked when she was done talking. "What's the town coming to?"

"Yes, well, I didn't charge them extra for the fist fight," she said, distractedly. "I suppose I should have..." she trailed off, looking at him. He hadn't changed much, same old droopy moustache, baggy clothes, sallow complexion, satchels under his bloodshot eyes, unkempt hair, yellow teeth...

"Look, Mabel, I know I was an asshole to leave the way I did, but I've been thinking about it..."

"Me, too," she said, continuing her survey: scuffed up shoes, whiny nasal voice...

"And, like, if you could give me another chance..."

"Sure, honey; we'll go ice skating in hell, okay?"

"Yeah, baby, that would be great," Eddy said with a sneer masquerading as a smile. "And then we can— Who the fuck is looking for you on a Sunday, Mabel?"

"Who isn't? Maybe it's the Jehovah's Witnesses," she said, waving them to go into her bedroom. "This won't take long, I don't understand enough Spanish to be converted. I think you know everyone." Before she closed the door, she noticed Anna in deep consultation with Bobby, Paula and Suzy; Ross was thumbing through a copy of "The Nation" magazine, but put it down to greet Eddy; Carlos had her Walkman headphones on and was listening, she assumed, to the Miles Davis Quintet tape in it. Everybody seemed occupied so she went to get rid of whoever was at the door now.

She opened it on Frank and Belinda having a screaming fight on her doorstep. "Ah, the romance progresses," she thought, but said, "Get the fuck in here before you freak out the neighbors!"

"Hackenbush, will you tell her that Charles is no good for her and to come to Vegas and marry me today!"

"Charles is no good for anyone, Belinda, go to Vegas and marry Frank. How'd you find me anyway?" Hackenbush asked, lighting a cigarette.

"I had you investigated when I thought..." Seeing

Hackenbush's face, Belinda trailed off. "When I thought you might be able to, ah, help me and Frank."

"Find anything interesting about me?" Hackenbush asked, getting over her shock. She was now amused by the girl's discomfort.

"Um, no, actually, you've never been arrested or in any kind of scandal," Belinda admitted.

"What were you looking for in my past, Belinda?" Hackenbush asked, intrigued now.

"Something we could use against Charles," Frank said quickly.

"I see," she said. "However, there's nothing incriminating or embarrassing enough my past to use against him because I've always steered clear of your kind of people." She blew some smoke at them and told them to get out.

"Hackenbush, I'm sorry," Belinda said, standing her ground. "Frank brought me here to try to convince me...well, never mind, I am sorry that we tried to involve you. I'll just have to accept my fate and marry Charles."

"Or you could run off with Frank and accept that fate," Hackenbush said, moving toward the door. "Charles is terrible dancer anyway. Or you could dump them both and get a real job and see what fate is really like. Or you can go straight to he– I'm so popular today I can hardly stand it." She leaned against the door.

Belinda glanced out the window and gasped. "That's Charles's Mercedes," she hissed. "Is there a back way out?"

"Honey, you definitely should not be marrying someone whose car scares you that much," Hackenbush sighed. "You can cower in my bedroom until he leaves; the party's in there anyway." She waved them into that room, squared her shoulders and opened the door, something she would never have done in hell if there hadn't been all those people in her bedroom to (hopefully) rescue her if he got rough. "And to what do I owe the honor of a personal appearance?" she asked, closing the door and leaning on it.

"Guilt."

"Yours or mine?"

"Mine, Hackenbush, I was a cad–"

"And a swine."

"Yes, and—"

"And a bastard."

"Yes—"

"And a hound."

"And, I'm here to apologize," he said, standing erect.

"Thanks, that's very nice of you; I suppose you know how to get to the freeway?" she asked, opening the door again.

"And I love you," he said, closing the door and leaning on it.

"And you're marrying Belinda."

"That has no effect on us," he said in his most convincing lawyer voice. "I'm sure I could make you very happy."

"What are you offering me here, Charles?"

"Comfort, security, love."

A cage, a leash, your dick. "No sale, fella."

"I'm not trying to buy you, Hackenbush."

"Oh sure you are, Charles, but what all you guys got to figure out is that there is much in this world you can never buy, let alone own." She strolled over to her bedroom door, opened it and beckoned Belinda and Frank to come out. "Maybe I'm old-fashioned, Belinda, but it seems a little odd to me that your fiancé is trying to set up a mistress before he marries you."

"What the hell are you two doing here?" Charles had gone white with rage.

"I don't know if you still need a reason to be embarrassed, but, well, this could be it," Hackenbush said, staying focused on the girl. "Or what about a reason to be enraged, Belinda? This is how little we both matter to him; he'd make possessions out of both of us, love us the same, which can't be much if it's spread so thin, and how long before the embarrassing rumors start to fly? But by that time, will either of us have any will left to leave him or will we just stay while he grinds us into nothing? Is that the life you want, Belinda? Because even if I say no, they'll be someone one else saying yes pretty soon; I'd bet money on that."

Frank had moved protectively between the women and

Charles, but both he and his half-brother were frozen listening to Hackenbush's recital of Belinda's future.

Belinda exhaled a long breath and slumped a little. She twisted a huge hunk of ice off her left hand and, gently pushing Frank aside, held the ring out to Charles. "I'm going to Las Vegas to marry Frank, Charles; I love him and I don't love you," she said in a thin but firm voice.

Hackenbush winced mentally; whatever she thought of Charles, those words had to hurt. Momentarily she considered giving back her fancy monogrammed lighter, but Belinda would probably get another hunk of ice from Frank, who was also loaded, and Hackenbush had no idea where the next fancy monogrammed lighter might be coming from. If another one ever was, that is. "Now, get out, Charles; and don't let the security door hit you on the ass on your way out," she said, bored with the whole scene already.

Charles put the engagement ring in his pocket, turned on his well-polished heel and left. Frank turned and gave Hackenbush's arm a squeeze and told her she was his hero. She told them to get out and they did. When they were gone, Hackenbush sighed and went into her bedroom.

"That was brutal, Hackenbush," Ross said, looking slightly ill.

"Wasn't it? I didn't even enjoy it." She looked at the skeptical faces around her. "Well, okay, just a little. But I can't stand that society trash, can you?"

Everybody said no, they couldn't, and got up to leave. Ross and Carlos waved and said they'd see her later. Bobby took her aside and looked deeply into her eyes. "Hackenbush, I..."

"What is it, Bobby? You can tell me."

"I was wondering..."

"Yes?"

"Where do you get your glasses?"

"Frame and Lens; they're called 'Fifties' and they're forty-nine ninety-five including the lenses," she said with much gravity.

"Thanks, doc!" he said, bounding out the door after Suzy, Anna and his mom.

"What a great kid," she thought, turning to face the Eddy Lee situation. Cody and Shorty looked on sympathetically; Gregg seemed a little hostile, as if he thought she'd offer Eddy his job if he left the room. On the other hand, he'd come there with Shorty and Shorty looked rooted on the spot. "So, Eddy, here's the deal; I'm done with you," she said quietly. "Maybe if you'd come back two or three years ago, then maybe we could've gotten together. But four fucking years is a long time and I'm over you. I loved you, you left me, it hurt, it was painful, but since I didn't die, I got over it. I just don't feel that way about you or the situation anymore. So you're wasting everybody's time here, dig?"

"No, I don't dig it, Mabel," Eddy said, and pointed at her nightstand. "If you're over me like you say, what about this?"

"What?"

"This!" He grabbed the picture of the two of them off it. Her reading lamp fell over.

"That? I forgot about that. It holds up the lamp." She took the frame from him and blew a cloud of dust off it. "Want it? I'll get something else to hold up the lamp." She watched him shake his head. "Then hook it, Eddy, I have a busy day ahead of me. See ya, cats," she said as they filed out of her bedroom and out of her house.

Hackenbush took a deep breath and rolled her sore shoulders; they hurt, but they'd be okay. The song started up in her head again, so she picked up her new baritone ukulele and went back to her interrupted practice. She was looking forward to being back at the Lotus Room, drinking Ramos Gin Fizzes by the fabulous Wang, the drunks, lounge lizards, hipsters, music lovers, Hackenbush fans, and all the hustlin', scufflin' folk that lived in her world. Her true world, which had its own set of problems, but where there were no creepy bosses, no underlings, no clients, no petty harassment, no fake pleasantries, no suppressed rage or despair, no guarantees for the future or empty promises of security, no bitter coffee and stale donuts nobody wanted in the first place, and most importantly, no Republicans: just people living hand to mouth on or for their art and doing the best they could.

Ginger Mayerson

And so in this early spring of 1988, the United States was still wracked by AIDS, still had the waitress tax, still had no universal healthcare, was still just saying no to drugs with as much success as such a stupid idea like that would have, still had Ronald Reagan as president, and the rich were still getting richer, while the rest of us just got fucked and not even kissed; Hackenbush's life returned more or less to normalcy, whatever that might be.

The End

www.ingramcontent.com/pod-product-compliance
Lightning Source LLC
Chambersburg PA
CBHW071943170626
46813CB00005B/1814